searching for rescue

redwood coast rescue, book 1

Tonya Burrows

part one
lost

"Lost causes are the only ones worth fighting for."
Clarence Darrow

chapter
one

ZAK HENDRICKS WASN'T drunk enough for this shit.

He glared at his former best friend across the scuffed bar and knocked back another shot of Jameson. His fourth of the night. At *this* bar. He washed it down with a glug from his second beer.

Yeah, still not drunk enough to deal with Sheriff Ash Rawlings' holier-than-thou attitude.

"Whaddya gonna do, *Ashley*?" He leaned on Ash's full first name because he knew it bugged the guy, then signaled the bartender that he was ready for another shot. He'd told her to keep them coming until he was wobbling on his stool. Then maybe he'd be able to sleep tonight. "Arrest me for having a drink? I'm over a decade past the legal age. And I seem to remember *you* used to drink with Donovan and me long before we were legal. You used to be fun."

A muscle twitched under Ash's neatly trimmed beard. He hated being reminded of his wayward youth, so Zak delighted in mentioning it every chance he got.

"That was a long time ago, Zak. I grew up."

"And now you're the big, bad Sheriff of Lost County. The fun police."

"What you've been doing tonight is nowhere in the neighborhood of *fun*. I could arrest you for assault, destruction of private property, disturbing the peace... take your pick. You've had a busy night." Ash scowled and held up a hand, stopping the bartender from pouring another shot. "He's done, Rose."

"Not if he still has money, Sheriff. He's single-handedly keeping the lights on around here." Rose Galasso put a hand on her slim hip, and her cropped Mad Dog Pub T-shirt rode up to show a glimpse of a tattoo on her ribs.

Momentarily distracted from the conversation by the colorful ink, Zak wondered what the tattoo was and just how much skin it covered...

As fast as the spark of interest flared, it fizzled. Rose was a beautiful woman with breasts that tested the limits of her shirt, long black hair, and snapping blue eyes—but he only needed one lover in his life, and her name was Whiskey.

Who could've guessed his sex drive was in the leg he left back in Afghanistan?

Goddammit, he wanted another shot.

"Rose, my drink?"

Ash turned that sanctimonious glare on her. "Don't do it. I'll have your liquor license stripped for over-serving."

"Asshole," Rose muttered but set the bottle of Jameson down and walked away.

"This is bullshit. I didn't start that fight at the brewery." Zak shoved to his feet. The room tilted, the floor rolling under him. He stumbled sideways, and the toe of his fucking prosthetic leg caught on his stool. He crashed into a nearby table, sending a trio of backpackers scurrying to get out of the way. Glasses shattered; beer spilled. His head cracked against the floor as he landed, and his vision dimmed for a second, but he didn't feel any pain through the haze of alcohol and rage. The white-hot, all-consuming rage he couldn't drink away.

Rage at himself.

And at Rose for not giving him another drink.

And at Ash for trying to leash him.

And at his useless fucking metal leg for being useless and metal.

And at the men who brought him home broken instead of leaving him in Afghanistan to die a hero.

"Jesus," Ash said softly and reached down to help him.

He shoved Ash's hand out of the way and tried to stand, only to discover his prosthetic was no longer attached. It stood wedged in the footrest between the stool's legs. Face burning, he pulled himself upright on the table and hopped over to disentangle the prosthetic, but it wouldn't come loose.

With a growl of frustration, he picked up the whole stool, leg and all, and threw it across the bar. It slammed into the wall by the door, and several pictures clattered to the floor. The abrupt movement upset his equilibrium, and he hopped on his one leg to regain his balance before he fell again.

Rose stared, and her red-painted lips opened in a little O of surprise.

The backpackers snickered.

"A one-legged man hops into a bar..." one of them said, and the snickers turned to laughter.

He snapped up a beer mug from the nearest table and threw it at them. "Shut the fuck up!"

Ash grabbed his arm in a vise grip. "Enough. You're going home." He raised an eyebrow at Rose. "Unless you want to press charges for destruction of property?"

After a second, she closed her mouth and shook her head. "It's fine. Just get him out of here."

Ash sighed and all but carried Zak out. When he stopped to untangle the prosthetic leg from the stool, Zak snagged the bottle of Jameson still on the bar and took a long drink.

"Goddammit." Ash yanked it out of his hand, gave it to Rose, and then muscled him out the door.

The July night was brisk, the air heavy with a sea fog that curled around the streetlights on Main Street, dampening their yellow glow. Across the street, spotlit by the lamp directly in front of the closed grocery store, a kid of about sixteen sat in the open side door of a camper van straight out of the 1970s. Her long blond ponytail trailed over her shoulder in dreadlocks from under her hooded sweatshirt. She twisted the end of one dread as she sucked on a cigarette and watched them with wary eyes.

He'd seen eyes like hers before.

Eyes that had witnessed too much, too young.

Eyes like Tehani's.

Jesus.

He should've opened his throat and sucked down that entire bottle of Jameson while he had the chance.

Ash dumped him into the back of a Chevy Tahoe marked with the green and brown Lost County Sheriff logo and shoved the prosthetic leg at his stomach. "You're so goddamn lucky nobody's pressing charges tonight, man, or I'd be taking you to jail right now instead of home."

He leaned his head back against the seat and closed his eyes. "Doesn't matter."

Muttering a string of curses, Ash slammed the door shut and circled to the driver's side. He was still cursing when he slid behind the wheel. He didn't start the car. Instead, he sat there, opening and closing his enormous fists around the steering wheel.

Something snuffled at the back of Zak's hair. He bolted upright, twisting in his seat, ready to fend off an attack.

Intense golden eyes stared through the metal bars separating the trunk space from the rest of the vehicle. The dog

—*was it a dog?* —had a brindled coat, tall, pointed ears standing erect on its wedge-shaped head, and a black mask around those creepy gold eyes. Its lips peeled up, showing a row of vicious-looking teeth.

Zak leaned forward, away from its snarling snout. He got the feeling the cage separating them wouldn't do a damn thing if it really wanted to chomp down on his spine. "The fuck is that?"

Ash glanced over his shoulder. "That's Ranger. One of my sister's projects. Careful. He damn near took off my arm trying to wrestle him into the truck." He started the engine and pulled away from the curb. "A lost cause, you ask me."

Like you.

It went unspoken. It didn't need to be said. Zak was well aware of what everyone in town thought about "that Hendricks boy." Everyone, including his own family and his former best friend.

Tortured.

Damaged.

Trouble with a capital T.

A lost fucking cause.

"But you know AJ." Ash sighed heavily, his broad shoulders moving with the exasperated exhale. "The queen of lost causes."

He *did* know Anna Jade Rawlings. Far better than Ash knew. He wondered what the by-the-book sheriff would do if he detailed exactly *how much* of Anna he knew. Her flaming copper hair was all natural and matched everywhere—top and bottom. It also fit her personality. She was fiery and strong-willed and just as self-righteous as her twin brother. She was also generous to a fault and the most compassionate person Zak had ever met.

The queen of lost causes.

And even she didn't think he could be saved.

But apparently, she thought this bloodthirsty dog had a shot.

What did that say about him?

chapter
two

BELLA LOWE WATCHED the sheriff warily, but he had his hands full dealing with the drunk man. He wasn't worried about an underage girl out too late, smoking a cigarette.

It was a bad habit, she knew. But she also knew there were worse ones.

She looked down the quiet street with its charming Victorian storefronts to the eyesore on the corner. This town was cuter than others she'd visited, but underneath that quaintness was a seething underworld, and its epicenter was The Palace. Maybe the place had been a palace at one time—it looked the part, with all its ornaments and flourish—but now it was a peeling, sagging black hole that fed on the souls of the drug-addled and desperate. It reminded Bella of an aging hooker, past her prime, but still trying to paint herself attractive with bright colors and inappropriate clothing.

Mom had gone inside to score some meth hours ago. Jessica had either passed out in the bar or found a man willing to pay her for sex. Probably both. Knowing her mother, definitely both. Either way, she was on her own for the rest of the night.

Sighing, Bella stamped out her cigarette on the sole of her knock-off Doc Martens. The smoky mint of the menthol was making her nauseous. She hadn't eaten a decent meal in days, had been existing on gas station chips, soda, and one shriveled hot dog.

She sensed movement behind her and shifted to look at the bed stretched across the camper van's back half. Her sister sat up. With big blue eyes, wild blond hair, and chubby, dirty cheeks, Poppy was still little more than a baby. Barely five. Soft and still so innocent.

"Bella?" she said around a yawn. "I can't sleep. I'm hungry."

"I know, kiddo. Me, too." She glared down the street at The Palace. Mom wasn't coming out anytime soon, so what was the point of waiting around here?

She climbed into the van and shut the door. The overhead light turned off, plunging them into night's cool, damp darkness.

"Bella?" Poppy's voice was a tiny squeak. She'd always hated the dark.

"It's okay. Nothing in the dark can hurt you." Darkness was safety. It was a blanket to hide in—protection from Mom, who always left at night, and her mood swings. It was a refuge from the leering men that Mom liked, who always went with her when she left. Darkness was an invisibility cloak, allowing freedom from detection by the cops and the abusive shit of a man they'd spent the last several years running from.

Daylight was far more frightening.

The camper they called home was nothing more than a king-sized mattress they all shared and a short stretch of cabinets along the wall opposite the sliding door. Nothing was in those cabinets besides a few dishes, a dented stock pot, a hot plate they rarely used, and a camp lantern. Bella found the light and flipped the dial to turn it on. The battery was dying, but it was better than nothing. She set it on the counter beside a narrow sink.

"Scoot over."

Poppy shifted, making space on the bed. She sat beside the little girl and put an arm around her thin shoulders, pulling her in close.

Poppy wrinkled her nose. "You were smoking again."

"Yeah."

"Smoking's bad for you."

"Yeah, I know."

"Why do you do it?"

Probably for the same reasons Mom wasted her life flitting around the country, chasing men and her next high: an addictive personality, a deep need for love, a tendency for self-destruction, a disdain for convention. Bella was nothing if not her mother's daughter. If not for Poppy, she'd be Jessica Lowe's copy in every way.

Poppy's birth had saved her from their mother's fate.

The least she could do was feed the child.

"Tell you what. I saw a truck stop off the highway a ways back, and it had a Wendy's. Want nuggets?"

Poppy's face lit up. "And a Frosty?"

Bella thought of the crumpled five in her pocket that she'd been hoarding for two weeks. It was all the money she had left from the forty she'd taken from Mom's purse before Jessica smoked, injected, or snorted it all. Only enough for nuggets, but she couldn't say no to all that hope in Poppy's eyes.

"Sure. We'll even get some fries."

She'd figure something out. Maybe she'd get lucky, and it'd be a lonely guy working the late shift. She could exchange a blow job for the meal. Her stomach twisted at the thought, but it wasn't the first time, and it wouldn't be the last. She'd do anything to keep Poppy safe.

In that way, she was very much not like her mother.

Poppy's excitement faded, and she looked out the back window at the foggy street. "What about Mom? She told us to wait."

"Fuck Mom."

Poppy gasped, then smothered a giggle behind her hand. "You said a bad word."

She cupped the girl's face and waited until their gazes met. She wanted to make sure her next words were understood because she might not be around to protect her sister forever. Two more years, and she'd be eighteen, legally an adult. She'd do everything in her power to keep Poppy by her side when she finally left, but it might not be possible at first. She'd need a job and a place to live. She'd need to prove she was a better parent than their mom. Who knew how much time that would take?

"Listen, Pop. This is important, okay? You never, *ever* put Mom's needs before your own, no matter what she says you owe her. Because you don't owe her anything. Real moms are supposed to protect their kids, care for them—make sure they are safe and happy and comfortable—but she has never done any of that. She's never put you first. So if you're hungry, you get food, and fuck Mom. Let me hear you say it."

Poppy's eyes widened. "Fuck Mom," she whispered, gaze darting like she was still afraid she'd be reprimanded for the swear.

"Louder."

"Fuck Mom!" she shouted, then squealed with laughter.

"There you go." Bella got off the bed and slid into the driver's seat. She didn't have a license—needed money and a stable address for one—but she'd been driving the camper since she was tall enough to reach the pedals. As she cranked the key and prayed the engine started, tiny arms circled her neck from behind and squeezed.

"I don't need a mom," Poppy said and kissed her cheek. "I have you."

chapter
three

THAT LAST GLUG of Jameson had done the trick, thankfully shutting off Zak's brain and allowing him to drop into sleep during the long ride from town to his cabin on Bluff Road. He didn't remember Ash wrestling him out of the SUV or dumping him into bed. He didn't remember his former friend staring down at him with a disapproving frown, sad eyes, and a whispered, "What happened to you over there, man?"

All he knew was the floaty, buzzy peace of an alcohol-fueled sleep.

At least until the nightmares reached through the pleasant darkness and wrapped their boney hands around him, dragging him down into their oily muck. They always started the same—a rehash of the moment he fucked his life. He'd walked into a room at the abandoned U.S. base way up in the Hindu Kush, and saw a scared sixteen-year-old girl strapped into a bomb vest, trembling and white-faced and determined to pull out the wires until the vest exploded. She'd been willing to kill herself rather than become a martyr for her megalomaniac husband.

He crouched in front of her and caught her wrists. "Tehani, don't. It's not active."

She blinked at him like she didn't understand, even though he'd spoken in Pashto.

"It's not active," he said softly again. "I made sure it wouldn't hurt you."

He checked over his shoulder at a soft sound from the hall. Was that a footstep? Askar, Jahangir Siddiqui's second in command, was growing suspicious of him, and he knew that the unfeeling bastard was having him followed.

They were out of time.

He surged to his feet and scooped Tehani into his arms. She was so light—he'd carried heavier rucks—that he had her halfway out the window before she fought him. She sent a fist flying. He dodged it, but wasn't fast enough. It glanced off the side of his head and rang his bell enough that he nearly dropped her.

"Fuck!"

Tehani froze and stared at him, and he realized too late that he'd spoken in English.

"Who are you?" she whispered.

He switched back to Pashto and set her back on her feet. "You need to trust me."

At the sound of voices in the hall, he glanced toward the door and swore again. This time, he didn't bother to hide the English curse.

She shied away from him. "You're American!"

He gripped her shoulders, holding her still. "Tehani, do you want to leave here?"

She nodded, and her veil slipped off her head. Her dark eyes were huge in her too-thin face.

Tehani hadn't been his mission, but he couldn't leave her behind. He'd grown too attached to the feisty, stubborn girl in his months deep undercover, so when he discovered her husband's plan to kill her, he'd rigged the vest, making it inactive, then boosted her out the window. He followed, but landed badly and jacked up his ankle. He couldn't outrun the fighters chasing them, so he'd sent her on ahead with his intel and hoped it reached American troops in time. She escaped, survived, and thrived.

He... hadn't.

Pain.

It hit so bright and hot that it reached through his dreams into reality. Sweat beaded on his skin. His breath sawed in and out of his lungs. He twisted in bed, knotting the sheets under him.

As an Army Ranger, he'd trained to withstand torture, but no amount of training could prepare a guy for the reality of having his back stripped to ribbons with a cane. Over and over again, each strike worse than the last. Blow after blow until his voice gave out from screaming, and the copper-penny scent of his own blood flooded his senses, and his knees collapsed from under him. His body swung forward, catching on his bound arms, wrenching his shoulders nearly out of their sockets. Unconsciousness would've been a blessing, but he was too damn stubborn. He stayed awake through it all until they tired of the cane and continued the beating with fists and boots...

Zak bolted upright, gagging on a scream and the surge of liquor burning back up his throat. His stomach emptied in an eruption, splattering the floor beside his bed. When it was over, he fell back on the mattress and stared up at the spinning ceiling, shaking and sweat-slicked and cold down to the marrow of his bones.

He couldn't go back there.

No more sleep.

He fumbled in his pocket for the baggie of Stay Awake he'd bought from a dealer at The Palace earlier in the night, praying Ash hadn't searched him and taken it before leaving.

Still there.

He breathed out in relief and then smirked. Some cop Ash was.

He didn't bother with neat lines. He just dumped the fine white powder onto the back of his hand and snorted. The rush hit almost instantly, warming his blood, sizzling away the lingering dark slime of the nightmares. The shaking stopped. He felt awake, alive...

Invincible.

This was better. So much better.

He secured his prosthetic leg in place, then took another bump, relishing the hot euphoric buzz. It was the closest he'd been to happiness in two years. He could ride this wave well past dawn. Sleep was overrated.

He grabbed his motorcycle keys. July nights on the Northern California coast were cold and blanketed in fog, but the bike was his only option since his truck was still at the Mad Dog in town. And he sure as hell wasn't going to town. He wanted another run-in with Ash about as much as he wanted to go back to sleep.

He'd cruise up the mountain to Wildcat Ridge and watch the sunrise. If he got lucky, he might even find a party still raging on the Ridge and he wouldn't have to worry about running into Ash. The legalization of marijuana had made the mountain more volatile, and it was too dangerous for anyone in uniform to patrol up there alone. With more people vying for less money, the illegal farmers viciously protected their crops by any means necessary.

There was a reason locals called Mt. Humboldt "Murder Mountain." People often went up there and vanished.

None of that bothered Zak. He liked the mountain, the outlaws, and the backwoods justice. Everyone there was just doing their own thing, and if you didn't bother them, they wouldn't bother you. He wished more people in town were like that.

Why couldn't they let him destroy himself in peace?

The thought made him laugh, and he pushed the bike faster, nearly laying it down around the next curve in the road. Ocean fog had rolled in thick and damp, choking off visibility to only a few feet in front of his headlight. Each hairpin turn on Highway 1 became a death-defying adventure. What waited on the other side of the turn? A rock wall? A cliff dropping into the ocean? More winding road?

Did he care?

Nope.

He was flying.

He was free.

Nothing else mattered.

A pair of headlights suddenly pierced the fog, momentarily blinding him. An old camper van chugged up the hill from the opposite direction. He had time to get out of the way —plenty of time to swerve back into his own lane on the narrow road—but one thought crystalized from the buzzy haze in his brain.

This is it.

The escape he'd wanted for two long years.

Once, during a late-night PTSD-fueled phone call, his friend Greer Wilde asked if he ever thought of killing himself. Yes, all the time. It was constant, eating away at the back of his mind like a cancer.

"Why don't you do it?" Greer had asked.

"Same reason you don't," he'd shot back because he hadn't wanted to admit that he was a coward and too afraid to take that step.

But *this* wasn't suicide. This would just be a tragic accident. His family and friends would mourn, but they'd also be relieved. The town gossips would *tut-tut-tut* about that "poor Hendricks boy," but they'd be relieved, too.

It was better this way.

But in the heartbeat before the collision, he saw the driver's face—a ghostly, terrified oval in the splash of his headlight beam.

A girl.

Just a girl.

Like Tehani.

Jesus.

He wrenched the handlebars to the right, overcorrecting. The van clipped his back tire and sent him skidding across the highway. There was no guardrail. The front tire hit the narrow strip of slick grass along the shoulder, and the bike flipped out from under him. He sailed over the handlebars, tumbling through the air, aware that he was falling too far, too fast. He should've hit the ground by now, but the earth had vanished.

He'd gone over the edge of the cliff.

Any second, he'd hit the ocean and sink, broken, into its dark, cold embrace. He wasn't afraid. He'd gotten what he wanted, after all.

He was flying.

He was dead.

It *was* what he wanted...

So what the fuck was this panicked surge of regret?

When he finally landed, he wasn't greeted by the oblivion of the ocean like he thought. He hit a rock outcropping and felt a bone snap in his arm as he bounced.

No. No! Fuck, this wasn't what he wanted.

He flailed for something to grab, but his left arm was as useless as his missing leg. His prosthesis was gone. His helmet was gone—had he even been wearing one? Squat bushes reached for him with thorny hands and ripped his clothes, tore his skin. With the world tumbling around him, he had no sense of direction anymore. The road, the hill, the cliff's edge, the ocean. Road, hill, cliff, ocean. Road, hill, cliff, ocean. It blurred around him until, suddenly, it all stopped.

He landed on his back with his head uphill and the sheer drop of the cliff inches from the bottom of his boot. The fog, disturbed by his fall, swirled and then settled around him like a damp blanket. He couldn't hear anything. Couldn't feel anything.

Maybe he had died, and this was Hell. No sound, no feeling. Just endless gray.

Something small hit the top of his head. Then another. Pebbles pinged around him. He could hear again, too. Footfalls crunched on stone—someone was kicking the pebbles loose as they skidded down the hillside.

Zak tried to crane his neck to see, but pain swamped his senses and threw him back in time to Afghanistan. He'd never been rescued. His whole life for the past two years was only a figment of his imagination, and now Askar was coming back to torture him some more.

When hands touched him, he struck out at the ghostly figure in the fog. The female gasp of surprise caught him off guard.

Tehani?

Her face floated before his eyes. Not as she was then at sixteen—scared and too thin and still so stubbornly determined—but as she was now, a brilliant high school senior who already had a full ride to Stanford next fall. She lived down the street with his parents. They had sponsored her student visa at his request, then officially adopted her when they discovered she had no family left in Afghanistan save for a sister-in-law. She slept in his old bedroom and attended his high school with so many of the same teachers he'd had. He hadn't died for her, but he'd given her his life.

And he couldn't even look at her anymore.

Tears spilled in hot tracks from the corners of his eyes. He reached out a hand to her, surprised to see how bloody it was. Past and present blurred. He was simultaneously in Afghanistan, beaten and broken, and bleeding out on a cliff in California.

I'm sorry, he wanted to say, but something was blocking his throat. He tried to clear it and blood spilled from his mouth.

"Oh my God." She grasped his hand, and her face came into focus. "Oh, fuck."

Not Tehani.

The driver of the van.

This girl had the same brown skin, but her hair hung in long blond dreadlocks from under the hood of her sweatshirt. She had a nose ring and his gaze zeroed in on the small gold hoop. It sparkled when she spoke. "I'm so sorry. I'm so, so sorry. I didn't see you! I called for help. Hang on."

He wished he could tell her it wasn't her fault. He was the dumbass who tried to kill himself. She was just in the wrong place at the wrong time. But when he opened his mouth, more blood bubbled out rather than words.

"Oh, fuck," she said again and looked up as a police siren cleaved the fog. She tried to release his hand, but he held on tight. "Please. I can't stay. They're coming to help you, but I can't be here. I don't have a license. They'll take Poppy from me. I can't—"

He let her go as his strength faded. The last thing he saw before unconsciousness took him was the girl vanishing into the fog.

chapter
four

ANNA RAWLINGS BREATHED a sigh of relief as her twin brother's Tahoe stopped in the circle drive in front of her house. "You found him?"

Ash eased out of the driver's seat and circled to the back of the SUV. "Yeah, I got him."

She raced down the steps and reached him just as he pulled open the back hatch. Ranger sulked inside and glared at them with his bright yellow eyes. His lips curled off his teeth in warning.

"All yours, sis. I'm not touching him again." Ash stepped back and crossed his arms protectively over his chest.

Some big bad sheriff he was.

She rolled her eyes at him, then approached the kennel slowly, speaking to Ranger in a soft, soothing voice. "You're okay. Let's get you out of there now, huh?"

The dog relaxed marginally. He never fully relaxed, but she hoped to change that. After the hell he'd been through, he deserved a peaceful retirement. He allowed her to put the muzzle on him but wasn't happy about it. He all but steamed with resentment. "There you go. What a good boy!"

Ash snorted. "I think you need to look up the definition of good."

"Oh, no." She stroked her hand over Ranger's back and felt his muscles trembling under his beautiful brindle coat. "He's a very good boy under all of that snarl. He's just scared." She clipped on his leash and led him toward the barn next door to her house. "Where did you find him?"

"Going through the trash behind The Palace. I nearly got bit trying to wrangle him into the rig, then had to deal with a disturbance call at Mad Dog." He sighed heavily and rubbed a hand around the back of his neck as he followed her. "Zak."

He didn't need to elaborate. That name said it all.

She ignored the clench in her belly and kept her pace even. Feelings filtered down the leash, and she didn't want to stress Ranger out any more than he already was. But would she ever be able to hear Zak Hendricks' name without feeling a messy mix of... something? It had been fifteen freaking years since he took her virginity and bounced off to join the Army without so much as a see-ya-later. She shouldn't still care, but every once in a while, during her quiet moments, the hurt and shame crept back in to torture her.

And, dammit, she cared.

Zak was her first love, and despite what he'd done to her, witnessing his slow-mo self-destruction was painful.

She settled Ranger into a new run—a heavy-duty one this time, with cinderblock walls he couldn't chew through—then faced her twin again. "Thanks for finding him. And I'm sorry about Zak. I know seeing him like that hurts you."

Ash opened his mouth, but instead of saying anything, he shook his head and slung an arm over her shoulder. "I'm on break for the next twenty minutes. How about a coffee for your big bro?"

"You're fifteen minutes older."

"And fifteen minutes wiser."

She bumped her hip against his and felt his phone vibrate a second before it rang. "You're in demand tonight."

"So much for my break." He groaned and released her to slide the phone from his pocket. He answered with a brisk, "Rawlings."

"Want a to-go cup?" she whispered.

He nodded, but then his grateful expression shifted as he listened to the caller. It ran the gamut from anger to concern, then finally dread—all in the space of a heartbeat. Anna knew her twin's face as well as she knew her own. She could read him like a favorite novel. This wasn't a normal call-out. Something was very wrong.

"Where?" he demanded of the caller, and his strides lengthened. "Okay, I'll be there in ten."

She ran to catch up. "What happened?"

"A one-vehicle accident on Highway 1. Dispatch said a motorcycle went off the cliff."

Her breath stalled in her lungs. "You don't think—"

"I don't have to think. I know." He looked at her over the hood of his SUV, and in the warm yellow glow of her porch light, she saw a glint of tears in his eyes. "His truck was still at the Mad Dog. I drove him home."

She grabbed the passenger door handle as he slid behind the wheel. "I'm going with you."

"Anna, no. You—"

"He was my friend at one time, too." *And so much more.* She settled into the seat and crossed her arms mulishly, glaring at him, daring him to disagree. "I'm going."

Instead of arguing—her twin was a smart man and knew it would only waste time—Ash grumbled something under his breath and shoved the vehicle into drive. The ride was tense silence, broken only by the crackling murmur of his police radio until he hit the edge of town and flipped on his siren.

Highway 1 followed the coast, zigzagging while sandwiched between mountains and ocean. It was dangerous on a clear day. On a night like this, with fog smothering the countryside in a thick blanket, it was treacherous. The SUV's headlights barely penetrated the gloom.

"That's his bike," Ash said suddenly. He cut the siren and pulled his Tahoe sideways across the road, lights still flashing, reflecting garishly off the fog. The motorcycle lay in a twisted heap on the shoulder, but there was no sign of Zak.

Anna jumped out and cupped her hands around her mouth. "Zak!"

No answer.

"Zak!" Ash's voice boomed, carrying farther than hers, but still not far enough. The fog muffled everything. Still, they both waited for a breathless beat, hoping for a response.

Nothing.

Her stomach cramped with dread. What if Zak had gone off the cliff into the ocean? They'd never find him. He'd be lost forever. His poor family would never have closure—

No.

She shut down that line of thought. Nothing was lost forever. She *would* find him. She looked at her brother. "I'll go home and get Winston. He'll find Zak's body." Her golden retriever had trained for search and rescue since he was a puppy and had an incredible find record. He wouldn't let her down now.

"Take my truck." Ash grabbed a toolbox from the back, then tossed her the keys.

It was only as she slid into the driver's seat that she realized she was already thinking of this as a recovery mission.

Zak's body, she'd said.

Not Zak.

Not alive.

Something tore open in her chest, and tears flooded her eyes. Despite everything, the man was a hero. Damaged and twisted by war, but he still deserved better than this ending. She tightened her hands on the steering wheel and drew a breath, forcing back the tears. She needed to get Winston but couldn't bring herself to lift her foot off the brake. She watched Ash light a flare and drop it on the road. The phosphorous-red glow reflected off something metal in the grass as it fell.

Anna hesitated, then shut the SUV off and climbed out. An old, dented stock pot sat upright in the grass on the side of the road, like someone set it there intentionally.

Weird.

She picked it up, and her hand came away red. For a heart-stopping moment, she thought it was blood, but it was too waxy between her fingers. Lipstick? Someone had drawn an arrow pointing down the hill, away from the road.

Anna looked around, but the fog was too damn thick to see more than a few feet in any direction. She used the flashlight on her phone to scan the hillside, and the beam reflected off something farther down.

A helmet.

Zak's helmet. She could tell by the smiley face on the side. He'd told her once that his nickname in the military had been Smiley because he had smiled through everything the Army threw at him.

Until he returned home two years ago and stopped smiling altogether.

The helmet also sat upright, like someone had deliberately marked the spot with it. The yellow emoji winked in her flashlight beam under another lipstick arrow.

She followed and found a prosthetic leg arranged with the foot pointing down the hill. Another arrow. Beyond, a dark shape lay motionless in the grass.

"Ash, I found him!" She started down the hill, slipping in the slick grass and dislodging small rocks under her boots. She had to take a minute and slow down, or she'd slide right over the edge of the cliff. She sat and scooted the rest of the way on her butt.

He was...

Oh, God.

There was blood everywhere, soaking the front of his T-shirt under his leather jacket. His face was bruised and swollen, his eyes open to slits and unfocused. His left arm was broken, twisted unnaturally.

Her hand shook as she searched for a pulse. As soon as she touched him, he flinched away like he was trying to escape and made a sound that was all animalistic fear, reminding her of the abused dogs she rescued. This was not the cocky bad boy with the beautiful smile who stole her heart in high school.

She released a choppy exhale and impatiently swiped at the tears leaking from her eyes. "Shh, Zak. It's Anna. You're okay."

He tried to say something, and blood bubbled from his mouth. Shit, he was bleeding internally. He needed paramedics and a hospital.

"Ash!" She looked up the hill, searching for her brother, and started to get to her feet. In a lightning-fast move she wouldn't have guessed him capable of, Zak grabbed her hand so hard the bones in her fingers shifted.

"Can't... go... back..."

She dropped to her knees beside him. "You're not going anywhere except a hospital."

His gaze locked on hers, and the desperation she saw there broke her heart.

"Help," he whispered. "Help... me..."

"I will," she promised as his hand went limp and his eyes rolled back.

An ambulance siren whooped from the road, and she breathed a sigh of relief.

"Anna?" Ash called.

"Down here!" She found she couldn't release Zak's hand until the paramedics muscled her out of the way. She was too afraid the contact was the only thing holding him to this world.

"Hey." Ash wrapped an arm around her shoulders as the paramedics carried Zak up to the road. "Hey, don't cry. He's a fighter. He'll be okay."

She burrowed into her brother's side, inhaling the comforting scent of him, and didn't point out that he sounded like he was trying to convince himself.

Help me.

If Zak died, that plea, and the fearful desperation in his eyes, would haunt her for the rest of her life.

Help me.

And if he lived, she was going to fulfill her promise. Whether he liked it or not.

chapter
five

Six Weeks Later

BELLA WASN'T PREPARED for the storm. It came, as it always did, out of the blue. She'd sent Poppy to the neighbors to play with their adorable twin girls and was thrilled to have a few hours of quiet time. She'd found a book with a gorgeous cover that someone had left behind at a campsite and had been sneaking chapters at night after Mom and Poppy were asleep. It was a sweeping fantasy with a brooding dark fae prince, and an ordinary human girl swept up in the danger and intrigue of the fairy world. She couldn't wait to see how it ended.

But then the storm came.

It started with the slam of a car door.

She looked up from the book and saw Mom, who hadn't come home last night, get out of a beat-up old truck. A greasy man with a drug-scarred face sat in the driver's seat. He didn't look like he was awake enough to drive, but he shoved the clunker of a truck into reverse and dug holes in the ground as he peeled out.

The sound of the tires made Bella think of that foggy night six weeks ago and the man on the motorcycle. A few days after the accident, she'd found a copy of the local newspaper that someone had left on a picnic table. It said he'd been transferred an hour away to the nearest trauma hospital, but she had heard nothing since then.

She really hoped he was okay.

"Where's Poppy?" Jessica's eyes were too bright and ping-ponged around the campsite. She tore open the door of their van and flung their blankets onto the ground. "Poppy!"

"Wait, Mom. It's okay. She's not in there, but she's safe." Resigning herself to the fact she would not be finishing her book this afternoon, Bella closed it and pushed out of the camp chair she'd been lounging in. The chair was broken, with only her weight holding its legs in the right place. When she stood, it collapsed into the dirt.

Just like her life—held together with duct tape, gravity, and a prayer.

She exhaled hard and followed her mom into their van, picking up everything Jessica had tossed out as she went. "Mom, please stop. She's safe. She's playing with the kids from the next campsite over."

"You let her go *by herself*?"

"It's fine." She dumped the blankets in the passenger seat. Now she had to scrounge up change for the laundromat in town. She wasn't about to let her sister sleep in a dirty bed. "I know the family. The Whelans from Utah. They've been here for two weeks, and they're nice. Mr. Whelan works in tech, and Mrs. Whelan is a teacher, and they have twins, Sadie and Millie. They're leaving tomorrow, and the girls wanted Poppy to spend the day with them. They've become really good friends."

"How many times have I told you, you can't trust *anyone*?"

"I know, I know, but it's good for Pop to be with kids her age for once."

Jessica wasn't listening. She crashed out of the van. The door banged shut behind her, nearly catching Bella's hand.

Shit. This was bad. She had to get to Poppy before Mom.

She scrambled for the handle, hands shaking from the sudden adrenaline surge, but by the time she got out, Jessica was already storming back to their campsite with a crying Poppy in tow. Her grip would leave finger-shaped bruises on that tiny, fragile arm.

"Mom, don't. Please. It's not her—"

Jessica threw Poppy into the van and slammed the door shut. "You stay in there until I say you can come out."

"Mom, please—"

Jessica whirled on her. She never saw the backhand coming. She should've, but for some reason, she was always surprised when the abuse happened. Maybe because it wasn't a regular thing, and there was never any sign it was coming— no red flags. Mom had hit her while high and while sober, while angry, and even when she was calm.

Metallic blood filled Bella's mouth. Her lip had split. She swiped at the blood with her hand and tried not to look at Mrs. Whelan, who stood at the boundary of their campsite and watched with her arms crossed and a worried frown.

Jessica turned on her next. "Mind your own business, you nosy bitch."

Mrs. Whelan's shoulders straightened. She gathered her girls, who had come out to see what all the noise was about, and they disappeared into their huge, fancy RV.

"Mom, it's okay," Bella said, but Jessica was on a rampage.

Nothing would get through to her until the rage faded. She stomped around their campsite, kicking over their chairs and dumping the jugs of water Bella had carried from the pump for washing up. Water splashed over her book.

"No!" She lunged for it, tried to save it from getting too wet, but of course, that drew Mom's attention.

Jessica picked it up and looked it over. "What is *this*? Smut?" She ripped out a handful of pages and threw them at Bella. "Disgusting little whore." She shredded the book.

Bella scrambled to pick up the pages, clutching them protectively to her chest, then realized Mom wasn't standing there anymore. She was at the van's door, reaching for the handle, screaming at Poppy to shut up.

No. Not Poppy. She didn't deserve their mother's wrath.

Bella shoved to her feet and let all the anger and hatred inside her boil over. "*I'm* the whore? At least I only read about sex. You'll open your legs for anyone who will give you your next high!"

"You bitch!" Jessica flew at her with bruising fists, biting nails, and pointed shoes that felt like knives in her stomach and side.

Poppy continued to wail from inside the van, adding to the chaos, and she folded herself into a ball, covered her head with her arms, and wished she'd been born into a nice family like the Whelans. Instead, she'd gotten Jessica and a deadbeat father who disappeared when she was only a toddler.

She had flashes of her dad sometimes, usually in dreams— a black man with a big grin and booming laugh who had handled her gently. Those bits of memory were probably more fantasy than reality, but she clung to them anyway. Her dad loved her and only left because Jessica made him, or scared him away, or something.

And, like that, the storm passed, leaving silence and destruction in its wake.

She still didn't move, not fully trusting it was over until she felt her mother sit beside her. She lifted her head from her knees. Jessica wrapped an arm around her, and she forced herself not to flinch at the touch. She didn't want to do anything that might spark the storm again.

"I'm so sorry, Belladonna." Jessica buried her face in

Bella's shoulder. Tears fell on her skin and burned like acid. She wanted to shove the woman away, but that would only set her off again, so she stroked a hand over her mom's head instead.

Jessica sobbed. "I get so scared, you know? Jake is out there looking for us and could snatch Poppy away anytime. He still has custody. He can take her, and the cops won't do a damn thing to stop it because he's one of them! You *know* what he did to her. He *touched* her. I won't let him have her to ruin."

"It's okay, Mom." Her voice came out thin, and even she could hear the edge of fear in it. She cleared her throat and tried again. "I know you just want to protect us."

"Oh my God, I'm such a terrible mom."

"No." Bella nearly choked on the protest and told herself she had to perform better than this if she wanted any chance at a peaceful night. Jessica *was* an awful mom, but she supposed, in the grand scheme of things, there were worse ones out there. And it wasn't like she could trade her mom for a better model, like a car.

She had to work with what she'd been given.

And she'd been given Jessica.

She sucked in a breath and injected as much sincerity into her tone as possible. "You're not a terrible mom. You want to protect us. Bad moms don't protect their children."

Jessica smiled. "That's right. I'll do *anything* to keep you safe."

Except get a job. Or get an apartment. Stop using drugs. Stop hanging out with burned-out creeps like the one who dropped her off. Stop hitting us whenever the mood strikes.

A page of the book fluttered by, dancing on the salty ocean breeze.

Bella had to swallow hard to dislodge the knot of resentment. "I know."

Jessica popped to her feet. Her boho shawl with the bright southwest print and fringed edges swirled around her. "We've stayed here too long—time to hit the road and go north to Seattle. You'll like it there. Their music scene is lit. Or maybe east to the Rockies and Denver. Road trip! New town, new adventure."

Bella squeezed her eyes closed. Not again. Road tripping wasn't an adventure when it was all they ever did. At this point, the real adventure would be a house and school—a regular life.

Besides, they couldn't leave now. Bella finally had a lead on an under-the-table job she could do without a work permit. She'd also signed Poppy up for school with Mrs. Whelan's help, which started soon. She liked it here. She'd fallen in love with the soaring trees, craggy cliffs, and crashing ocean in the past six weeks. This part of the California coast was the most beautiful place she'd ever seen—and she'd seen a lot of the country in her sixteen years.

But she had to tread carefully with Mom or risk another storm. Make her think staying was her idea.

"That sounds awesome," she said, voice bright, almost chirpy. "But maybe not the Rockies right now. It'll be winter soon. All that snow. It's probably already snowing in some places up there. Seattle would be cool, but doesn't it get like a ton of rain?"

Jessica winced. "We'll go back south. San Diego."

"That puts us only a few hours from Jake. I don't want to be that close to him."

"Well, then, where do you suggest?"

She pretended to think about it for several seconds. "We're still safe here. You haven't seen Jake around or anything? He doesn't know we're here?"

"No. He can't possibly know."

"Wouldn't we be easier to track if we're on the road?

There are cameras all over. He'd know how to find the footage. And he probably asked his cop friends to watch the highways for anyone who looks like us."

It took a minute, but the light clicked on in Jessica's drug-addled brain. "He'll be looking for us in cities. He probably expects us to go to Seattle or Denver."

"Small towns like this are safer," Bella agreed.

"How did you get to be so smart?" Jessica slung an arm around her shoulder again and hugged her too tightly. "Okay, how about this? We'll stay here through winter and figure out where we want to go next in the spring."

"And maybe... we can find an apartment for rent?" She was pushing her luck. She knew she was but couldn't help herself.

Jessica's eyes flashed with temper. "What, our camper isn't good enough?"

"It's just... it might be cold over the winter. For Poppy, I mean. I don't mind it. Just thought—"

"What, you want a fancy RV like that flashy house on wheels next door?"

"No, I was only thinking of Poppy. I—"

Jessica shoved her. She wasn't braced for it—let her guard down again, dammit—and fell back, whacking her head on the camper's fender hard enough that she saw stars.

When she righted herself, Mom was gone.

She scrambled to her feet and made sure Jessica really had left before opening the van and climbing into bed beside her sister. Her entire body hurt. Her ribs ached, and a sharp pain stabbed through her chest every time she drew a breath, but it didn't matter. She'd take a million more blows if it protected Poppy from having to endure even one.

Poppy had sobbed so hard that she'd given herself the hiccups. As expected, she had a hand-shaped bruise on her thin arm. "I wish Mrs. Whelan could adopt us," she said between hiccups.

Bella wrapped the little girl up in her arms. She wasn't about to admit she wanted that, too, with all her heart. From this angle on the bed, she could see straight into the Whelans' RV. The twins were at the table, happily chattering away while they ate lunch. Mrs. Whelan's face appeared in the window, peering out between the blinds, the worried frown still pulling down the corners of her perfect mouth.

Bella pulled the ratty shade down, plunging them into a familiar, cozy darkness. She didn't want to see the other woman's worry or pity.

She tucked her sister's head against her sore chest and nuzzled Poppy's hair, which was freshly washed and braided and smelling of strawberries, thanks to Mrs. Whelan. "We'll be okay, Poppy. I promise you; we'll be okay. We have each other, and that's all we need."

chapter
six

PROBATION.

License suspended.

Enrollment in an outpatient drug and alcohol treatment program.

Zak only half-listened as the judge listed off his punishments like a god giving out commandments. He was too aware of the disappointed, disapproving gazes on the back of his head. His parents and siblings. Ash and Anna. He wished they had all stayed away.

Mandatory therapy for PTSD.

One hundred hours of community service.

It was bullshit. The only person he'd hurt was himself, and he'd already spent the last six weeks recovering from the broken arm and punctured lung with minimal drugs for pain management. Because, God forbid, they feed the junkie's habit.

He wasn't a junkie. He just wanted... oblivion. Was that so much to ask?

His lawyer patted him on the back and congratulated him. "It could've been worse. You'll be able to apply to lift the license suspension once you complete the treatment program." Then he turned and shook Grady Hendricks' hand and said the same thing.

At that moment, Zak hated his father for hiring the man. He'd been ready to plead guilty and face whatever punishment the court saw fit. He deserved it. Every time he closed his eyes, he saw a face, pale with terror in the splash of his headlight. He could've killed someone besides himself.

"Zakir."

His mother's soft voice had a surge of tears rushing to his eyes. He wanted to turn to her, fall into her arms, and breathe in her orange blossom perfume. He wanted her to comfort him like she always had after a nightmare when he was a child, but then she said in Pashto, "Please come home."

And he remembered the nightmare was his life now.

His skin crawled. The language used to make him think of home and comfort. It used to remind him of laughter at his American father's bumbling attempts to learn it and of his mother's fierce love, but it was the same language his torturers had used.

"Who are you, traitor?" Askar grabbed a young woman and her toddler, civilian prisoners, and shoved her into the chair across the Zak's. His left eye was swollen shut, and his right had been taped open so he wouldn't miss a second of the gore. They'd given up on torturing him, realizing that no amount of pain they inflicted would make him talk. Instead, they'd started hurting innocent people. Villager after villager dragged in front of him, shot and shoved aside. But the mother and child were too much.

"Don't," Zak whispered around the lump in his throat.

Askar pressed the gun to her temple. "Who do you work for?"

Zak almost broke. He opened his mouth to spill it all, tell them everything. He could take all the pain and humiliation they dished out, but he could not sit idly by while women and children were murdered in cold blood.

But the look on Askar's face as he held the gun to the woman's temple stopped him from uttering a sound. The little boy and his mother were both already dead in that soldier's eyes. They all were, and nothing Zak said would change that fate. He could spill all the state secrets he knew, and he still wouldn't save any of them.

"You fucking prick!" Tapping into a reserve of strength he didn't know he had, he kicked out with his chained legs. He unbalanced his chair, but he also nailed Askar in the balls, and the bullet meant for the woman went into the ceiling.

"Run!"

She didn't listen. She clung to her child, sobbing in big hyperventilating gulps.

After a moment, Askar straightened. Wincing in pain, he ignored the woman and child and limped over to Zak's over-turned chair. Still, there was no flicker of emotion. No anger, just a flat assessment. "Why risk death to save a woman you don't know?"

Zak gritted his teeth. The fall had sent his already-aching body flying to new heights of pain, but he wasn't about to let on how much damage he'd done to himself. He met the soldier's impassive stare with as much defiance as he could muster. "If you don't already know the answer to that, then you're incapable of understanding and I'd rather not waste my last breath explaining it."

"So you know," Askar said, "you didn't save the woman or her son." And he pressed gun's barrel against Zak's kneecap.

Bang!

Zak flinched and shoved out of his chair, the legs scraping loudly in the sudden silence. "I'm free to go?" he asked the lawyer, careful to keep his gaze away from his family.

"Uh..." The lawyer slid a glance toward his dad. "Yes. You'll have to report to your probation—"

"Yeah, I got it."

"Zak," his dad said. "Let me take you home—"

He shook off the hand Grady set on his arm and strode out. He'd thought the sound of the gun had been in his head, but discovered the heavy door loudly closed every time someone exited the room.

Bang!

Just a door.

Cold sweat had his shirt clinging to his spine by the time he stepped outside. He gulped in a lung full of cool autumn air and shook out his hands. His fists had been so tightly clenched his fingernails had left angry half-moon imprints on his palms.

"Zak, wait!"

Jesus, why couldn't they just let him escape?

He growled and spun to face Anna Rawlings. He must have looked feral because her protective twin, walking a half-step behind her, shoved her behind his body.

Like Zak would ever hurt a woman. Yeah, he was a bastard, but he had some lines he wouldn't cross. "What do you want?"

Ash plucked a folded sheet of paper out of Anna's hand and, ignoring her protests, shoved it at Zak's chest. "Your community service starts in one hour."

Zak took one look at the court order, snarled, and shredded it.

Well, okay. That didn't go over well.

Anna released a breath and bent to gather the pieces of

paper. She kept one eye on Zak as he walked away. His back was as straight as a steel rod, his movements stiff as if he still experienced pain from the accident. He was too thin, almost gaunt. Like a mean, feral street dog, wasting away but too distrustful of people to accept a helping hand.

"Are you sure you want to do this, AJ?" Ash asked with a heavy sigh and knelt to help her. "You don't need to put your reputation on the line for him."

But I promised I'd help him. She didn't say it out loud. Her brother was practical to a fault, a rule-follower with a strong sense of right and wrong and little tolerance for creative interpretations of the law. He was too jaded by Zak's antics these past two years and didn't think rehabilitation was possible, but it was *always* possible with enough patience and kindness.

At least, it was with dogs.

She had to believe it worked on people, too.

She *needed* it to work with Zak.

"You already have enough on your plate with those developers sniffing around the rescue," Ash continued, all practical reason. "Why take this on now?"

She ducked her head, hiding her wince. Monarch Development Corp. was more than sniffing around her land. They were taking her to court with a claim that her family never legally bought the land they'd been on for hundreds of years, and the presiding judge was the same one who just sentenced Zak, so her motives weren't entirely altruistic. Yes, Zak needed help. Yes, she thought she could help him. But showing the judge her rescue was worth more to the community than another resort would go a long way toward strengthening her case.

She straightened and faced Ash. "Someone has to believe in him, or he'll never believe in himself enough to seek help."

His gaze softened. "That someone doesn't always have to be you."

"Who else? *You*? You've given up on him." She waved a hand back toward the courthouse. "Did you see his family? They made the barest effort to connect. *They* are giving up on him. I won't."

"You have no idea what you've signed up for, but I can see there's no talking you out of it." Ash exhaled hard and gave her the pieces of paper he'd gathered. "Zak's poison. He's always been a little dangerous—I mean, look at the trouble he got me into when we were kids. But now it's—he's like a malignant cancer destroying everything he touches. He doesn't care who he hurts, and if he hurts you—" His voice cracked.

"I love you for worrying about me." She cupped one bearded cheek and raised to her toes to kiss his other. "But I'm stronger than you think I am. I got this."

"If he gets to be too much, remember there's no shame in backing out. They can easily reassign him to garbage duty with a highway crew."

It wasn't an option, but she couldn't let him know the truth—that she had to make this work or there was a very good chance she'd lose their family's land—so she simply nodded. "I'll keep it in mind."

Ash covered her hand with his, then stepped out of her reach as one of his deputies came out of the courthouse and called his name. He glanced in the direction Zak had gone. "He probably won't even show up. If he doesn't, he's in violation of his—"

"I know. I'll call you." She watched her brother walk away, then turned to look in the direction Zak had disappeared.

Please, please show up.

chapter
seven

HE DIDN'T SHOW UP.

Anna sat on the front steps of her house and stared down her driveway, willing him to appear even though Zak's first community service session was supposed to start nearly twenty minutes ago.

"Dammit!"

Winston bumped his head under her arm, and she smiled at her dog, scratching behind his floppy ear. "I'm okay, buddy. Just annoyed. It's like he *wants* to go to jail."

Winston licked her face. She hugged him, then sighed into his amber fur. "Guess I need to go call Ash and hear his I-told-you-so."

As she stood, Winston went on alert. He stiffened and stared intently at the driveway, then wiggled with excitement. She followed his gaze to the man standing on the street at the end of her long drive.

Zak.

He was here.

Late, but he'd taken the first step. He'd come to her. That was all she'd needed of him today.

"Well, look at that. He's here." She patted Winston's side and walked down the driveway, since Zak didn't seem inclined to take that second step yet.

He didn't look any better than he had hours ago at the courthouse. He'd always been a beautiful man with his bronze skin and thick, perpetually tousled black hair. He had dark eyes as rich as melted chocolate and lashes that any woman who had ever spent money on mascara would envy. The girls in school always thought he was a god, a perfect specimen all the other boys should aspire to be like, and he'd soaked up their adoration with his crooked half-smile and a naughty spark in his eyes.

That was the boy she remembered, the boy she'd secretly loved to distraction, but it wasn't the man standing before her. Those mischievous eyes were full of shadows and spoke of long, sleepless nights.

Haunted.

That was how she'd describe him now. Like he'd seen too many ghosts in his thirty-three years on this planet.

God, he was halfway to a ghost himself. The muscles those high school girls always swooned over were gone. He looked as if a good strong wind could topple him. His jeans hung on him, and then there was his leg...

She realized she was staring and pulled her gaze back to his face. "Thanks for coming."

His lips curled into an ugly sneer. "Like I had a choice."

She didn't flinch back. Just like with her dogs, she knew showing nerves now would be a game-ender. She'd get nowhere with him if he lost respect for her. "You did. Here or jail. I'm glad you chose here."

His snarl faded. After a beat, he crossed his arms over his chest. "Now what?"

"Why don't you come up to the house, and I'll get you something to eat? We can talk."

"I don't want to—"

She'd already turned away and started up the driveway at a brisk pace. If he wanted to complain, he had to catch her first.

She didn't glance back to see if he was following. She wanted to, but this whole thing was going to be a battle of wills, and she was just as stubborn as him. She refused to be the first to give in. She went inside to her kitchen and started pulling ingredients from the fridge for sandwiches. Deli meat, cheese, and an assortment of condiments. When she heard Winston's whimpers of joy from the porch—a typical golden, he loved new people—she let herself have a second of smugness. He'd followed.

She'd won the first war.

The screen door opened and slapped shut. A moment later, Zak stood in her kitchen. He may have been a shell of the man he used to be, but he still filled the small space with his presence, his dark mood charging the air. Winston didn't care. He tap-danced around Zak's legs, begging for attention. The man must have a heart of stone to ignore the dog's big eyes and infectious happiness.

"I don't want to talk," Zak finished. "I want to do whatever bullshit task I need to get you to sign off on my papers, then go home."

She set out four slices of bread and grabbed a butter knife from the cutlery drawer. "Where you can wallow in your misery in peace?"

"Something like that, yeah."

"Too bad. You're mine for the next four hours." She pointed at the table with her knife. "Sit. Do you like mayo or mustard?"

"I'm not hungry."

"Mayo it is."

He grumbled but didn't offer any other protest, so she took it as an agreement. She opened the jar and spread a thin layer on the bread, then added turkey, tomato, cheese, and lettuce. She made the sandwiches bigger than usual because he looked like he could use every calorie and finished the plate with a handful of potato chips and a thick pickle slice because back in high school, he could never resist a pickle. She set the plate in front of him, then went back to the fridge for two cans of sparkling water. As she bumped the door shut with her hip, she caught him staring down at his plate like a man who hadn't seen food in a very long time.

Her heart clenched. What happened to turn him into this? No, scratch that, she decided as she sat across from him and slid him the can of water. She really didn't want to know.

"Eat, Zak."

His hair was too long, having crossed the line from charmingly tousled to tangled mess months ago. He glared at her through the strands. "Why are you doing this?"

"Eating a sandwich? Because I'm hungry." She wasn't really, but she took a bite to make her point.

"No." He growled and shoved a hand through his hair, pushing it back from his face. "*This.* Sponsoring me."

"Would you rather be picking up trash on the highway?"

"No, I—" He stopped and seemed to struggle for words. A muscle twitched in his jaw under his thick layer of stubble. "You have every reason to hate me. Why help me?"

"Oh." Her stomach knotted, and she set down her sandwich. So they were going there now. She knew they'd have to talk about it but hadn't expected him to bring it up first thing. It was probably for the best to air it all out, but she wasn't ready. She dabbed her mouth with a napkin, giving herself precious extra seconds to gather her nerves, then met his gaze. "I did hate you."

"You still should."

"It was a long time ago." And she did *not* want to poke at those old wounds. She shrugged as if it was no big deal.

"Besides, I didn't have any attachment to my virginity. I wasn't saving myself for someone special or anything like that. I just didn't want to go to college a virgin, so if it wasn't you that summer, it would've been someone else." All partial truths, but he didn't need to know how deeply he'd broken her. He was dealing with too many demons as it was. She refused to add her own to the mix.

Zak swore viciously and pushed up from the table. He paced the few quick steps it took to cross her kitchen, then spun back. "I should've told you I had joined the military. I should've told you I was leaving before I ever touched you. And I should've said this years ago..." He trailed off and drew a breath. "I'm sorry."

Her jaw dropped open. Of all the things she'd expected from this meeting, an apology had been nowhere on that list. A hard knot rose in her throat, old sorrow returning to the surface. She should tell him...

No.

Look at him. He was barely functioning. Nowhere near healthy—physically or mentally—and he needed to be before she told him the whole truth.

It took longer than she would've liked to compose herself. "Uh, thank you, but it's fine. Really. Let's put it behind us and focus on getting you through this... uh, rough patch. Okay?"

He stared at her for several uncomfortable beats. "You've always been too nice."

"Why do you say that like it's a weakness? Our world could use as much niceness as it can get, don't you think?"

He scoffed but returned to his seat and picked up the pickle. He pointed it at her before taking a bite. "Nice people wind up dead."

"What about your parents? They're some of the nicest people I know."

He didn't respond. Just took another bite of the pickle and stared at her with those haunted eyes.

"Or are you talking about someone specific?"

The shadows in his eyes darkened. He glanced away.

"It's okay. You don't have to answer that. I'm not your therapist, but you will come here for your court-mandated therapy sessions with Dr. Firestone."

His gaze shifted back to her. "*Here*?"

"Yes. We're the only veteran treatment program in the county. We have group sessions on Wednesdays and dog therapy sessions on Saturdays. Some of our vets even volunteer here on off days. They find the dogs soothing and we've discovered the human-animal bond boosts the results of traditional therapy. You'll see some familiar faces."

He didn't respond. But, she noted with a zing of triumph, he'd picked up the sandwich. Baby steps. She gave him several minutes to eat before she spoke again.

"So," she said when he was almost done with the sandwich. "For me to sign off on your community service papers, you'll need to be here twenty-five hours a week for the next four weeks. You'll feed and walk the dogs, clean the kennels, help with set up and take down for group therapy, help with adoptions and doggy daycare, and assist with training."

"Is that all?" he muttered.

"Hey, this is *fun*."

"If you think picking up dog shit is fun, you need to reevaluate your definition."

"You could pick up highway garbage instead."

He grumbled and as expected, lost interest in the rest of the sandwich. He shoved the plate away and crossed his arms. He meant it to be a defiant, defensive gesture, but it also spoke of fear and vulnerability. He'd been afraid, on edge from the moment he stepped onto her property. If he knew how much of a glimpse into his damaged psyche he was giving her, he'd shut down completely.

So she had to make sure he didn't know.

She stood. "C'mon. I'll show you the facility."

chapter
eight

THE PROBLEM WITH SMALL TOWNS—OTHER than everyone knowing your business—was the past never stayed in the past. There was always something or someone around every corner to remind you of all the things you wanted to forget.

Like a first love.

A first heartbreak.

First fuckups and regrets.

Anna was supposed to stay in his past. He hadn't wanted to see her ever again. But now the woman he'd literally fucked over had become his jailer, the court-mandated key to his freedom.

Karma was a vicious bitch.

He followed Anna outside. The cheery yellow house with the big wrap-around porch had belonged to her parents, and it had changed little in the last fifteen years. He still remembered the distinctive creak of the porch swing from when he used to come over as a kid and play with Ash.

The Rawlings Ranch had been owned by the family since before the town was a town. Ash and Anna's parents used to have a thriving dairy farm, but after they died in a tragic car accident five years ago, the twins had sold off the cattle and torn down all but the biggest barn, which had been repurposed for Anna's dog rescue. With thirteen hundred acres stretching from ocean-front grasslands up into the timber-filled mountains, it was prime real estate and, recently, the town gossips had been buzzing about developers sniffing around the property. From the highest point, you could see the lighthouse to the south and Del Norte Beach to the north, as well as the sea stacks littering the coast. It was an awe-inspiring view.

It was also the first place Zak had kissed Anna.

It had been an abnormally warm spring day at the end of his senior year, with a clear sky made impossibly blue by a calm ocean. He'd gotten into a fight with his dad about joining the Army and stormed off to Rawlings Ranch to vent to his best friend.

But he hadn't found Ash.

Instead, Anna had been home alone.

As long as he lived, he'd never forget the way she looked, sitting on the front porch swing with a book in her hands and a glass of iced green tea sweating on the table beside her. Her dog, an old bloodhound with eyes as droopy as his jowls, snoozed in the sun, and she'd rub her bare foot lovingly over his back whenever she swung forward. Zak had seen her in shorts every summer, thousands of times, but he'd never *noticed* how long and gorgeous her legs were. She had a dainty chain around one ankle and sexy pink polish on her toes.

When had she grown up?

Desire hit him like a sucker-punch to the gut. He hadn't seen it coming, and his steps faltered as he approached her. He surreptitiously pressed a hand to the erection suddenly thrusting against his fly. What the hell was this? He couldn't get a hard-on for Anna.

It was *Anna*, for fuck's sake.

She barely glanced up from her book. "Ash is up on the hill helping Dad cut timber for the new barn."

The "hill," as she called it, was a mountain, and the main trail up was a moderately strenuous hike with an elevation gain of nearly fifteen hundred feet. Ash wouldn't be back until dark. His other best friend, Donovan, had stopped talking to him after their last brush with Steam Valley's finest had landed the three of them in jail for the night.

He had no one to talk to.

And he nearly popped off just from seeing Anna's legs.

Anna's.

Jesus. Maybe he was out of control, like his dad said.

He rubbed a hand over his face and sat on the steps with his back to her. "Shit."

"He isn't supposed to talk to you anymore, anyway. Dad thinks you're a bad influence."

"He's right. I am."

The swing stopped creaking. A moment later, she settled onto the step beside him, and he breathed in a lung full of sweetness, which didn't help the erection situation. He wanted to touch her and see if her skin was as soft as it looked. He wanted to undo her braid and run his fingers through all that fiery hair.

He popped to his feet and paced away, putting a safe amount of distance between them. "I should go."

"Hey, wait." She jumped up and caught his hand. "Are you okay?"

"Yeah, fine." He tried to shake her off, but she held on with surprising strength.

"No, really, Zak. What's wrong?"

"Just wanted to talk to Ash. No big deal."

"Well, you could try...." When she trailed off, he risked a glance at her. She gave an awkward shrug. "You could talk to me. I mean, you've known me just as long as you have Ash."

He couldn't tell her why that was such a bad idea. Couldn't let her know anything had changed between them. Because, for her, nothing had. This sudden sharp need was entirely one-sided.

"I'll go." He had every intention of leaving but made it only a handful of steps away before she spoke again.

"We could take the ATV up the hill. We might find him."

He turned back. "Your Dad won't like that."

"Dad'll get over it. You obviously need a friend right now, and since you won't talk to me, I'll help you find Ash."

She was too good. Too sweet. He should've walked away. The few warning alarms his teenage brain possessed were all blaring—*Danger! Danger! Danger!* —but he wouldn't learn to listen until the military fined-tuned those alarms into a sixth sense. So he climbed onto the ATV behind Anna and tried to keep their bodies from touching the entire ride up the hill.

It was torture.

And they didn't find Ash.

At the top of the hill, the entire world seemed to spread out at their feet. Anna sighed happily, climbed off the ATV, and wandered over to the edge to admire the view.

He admired the view of her.

It was a clear day with barely a cloud in the sky, but when she spun back toward him with a grin on her face, he swore he was struck by lightning. He didn't think. He wound his arms around her and pulled her in tight, thrilled that he could feel the flutter of her heart against his chest. She curled her hands into his shirt and stood up on her toes, and their lips touched. Gentle at first. Unsure and exploratory until the lightning struck again, sizzling between them, consuming them.

The kiss started a short, hot summer affair that ended the day he left for boot camp. He never told her he'd enlisted. He simply left because, at eighteen, it was easier to run off to war than face the complicated, messy crash of emotions he had for her.

And now he felt nothing.

Except...

As he followed her across the circular drive to a large A-frame building, his gaze skimmed down her backside, and he felt a tug of... something. It was too faint to name, but he'd been dead inside for so long that the sensation took him off guard. He miscalculated, and his metal knee locked up. He lost his balance, but Anna was suddenly right there, catching him before he fell.

Their gazes met, and that faint sensation in his chest coalesced into a spark, bright and inviting. It warmed him from the inside out, and for the first time in a very long time, he felt... *real*.

Alive.

For that moment, he wasn't a ghost trapped in night-mares, grasping for life with drugs and dangerous surges of adrenaline.

Amazed, he looked down at where she held his arm.

She let go. "Uh, sorry."

Why was she apologizing for touching him? He mourned the lost connection, which was weird when he hadn't wanted any kind of connection since returning from Afghanistan. "Nah, it's fine."

"Watch your step. The driveway's full of potholes."

He didn't see any potholes. She was giving him a plausible excuse for nearly falling on his face, and that pissed him off. He didn't need an excuse. He needed a new damn leg that didn't lock up every time he stepped wrong, but the VA was a slow-moving bureaucracy on its best days, so he wasn't holding his breath.

He strode forward with as much dignity as he could muster. "Let's get this bullshit over with."

chapter
nine

ANNA RARELY MISSED A BEAT, but he was almost to the barn-turned-dog rescue before she caught up. He'd surprised her—or, more likely, pissed her off.

Good.

The more distance between them, the better. He didn't need to feel anything. He preferred the numbness and had plans with a bottle of Jameson later.

She was all professional as she opened the front door and led him in. "Welcome to the Barn. We still call it that, even though it's not really a barn anymore with all the additions and renovations." She motioned to the room in front of them. It was painted a cheery blue and had bright pop art pictures of dogs on the walls. Centered on the back wall was a huge U-shaped desk, and an entire corner was dedicated to shelves filled with dog food, beds, leashes, and other pet supplies for sale. "This is the lobby, where we handle all the day-to-day stuff—adoptions, check-in for daycare, retail, etc. There's a room back behind the desk that we use for training classes and various community outreach programs. That's where you'll set up for group therapy. There's also a lounge with a TV and a kitchenette the staff uses as a break room." She pointed to the left. "That door leads through the play yard to our vet's office. Do you remember Sasha LeBlanc from school? She was a year behind us."

The name brought to mind a quiet, chubby girl with dark hair, pale skin, and even paler eyes behind oversized glasses. "Yeah, everyone called her Wednesday Addams."

"Only the jerks."

Zak said nothing because, yeah, he had been one of the jerks who called her that. But it was a well-documented fact he was an asshole.

"She's the best vet in town now," Anna continued, chattering a bit too brightly. "She rents the building next door, but her practice is fast outgrowing the space. I wish I could add on for her, but there's no money. She'll have to move to a bigger place eventually, and I dread the day. I'll take you over there and introduce you to her staff, but first, the dogs." She spun, and all but skipped into another hallway, her ponytail swinging in a mesmerizing arc between her shoulder blades. "We have forty-eight kennels arranged in three wings. A Wing is for our adoptable dogs. B Wing is our biggest. It's our long-term stay and doggie daycare. Then we have C Wing. It's reserved for my babies who need a bit more love before they can go up for adoption."

Of course, she pushed through the door marked C Wing. "This is where I'll need the most help. These dogs require extra training and socialization, so you'll be spending a lot of time in here."

The hallway was lined with ten large dog runs, but only three were occupied. The first was a golden retriever missing a large swath of amber fur across her back and shoulders. She shied away when he stopped in front of her kennel, shrinking into the soft bed in the corner with her tail tucked between her legs. Her brown eyes were bright with fear as she looked back and forth between them.

"That's Matilda," Anna said softly at his side.

"What happened to her?"

"Some sadistic asshole tied her to a tree this summer and set her on fire. Luckily, a group of hikers were in the area and heard her. They doused the fire before it did too much damage and brought her to Sasha. She's been here recuperating since. She's especially afraid of men, which leads us to think a man did this to her."

"The guy wasn't caught?" He realized his hands had curled into fists at his sides and forced his fingers to relax. Yes, he was an asshole, but he'd never harm an innocent animal like this. That took a special kind of evil.

"No. But the great thing about dogs is they don't live in the past, so we try to follow their example around here. Matilda has so much love to give. She just needs to learn to trust again, so it's a good thing you're here to help her overcome her fear. Most of my volunteers are women."

"I'm not a volunteer."

"But you are a man, and exactly what she needs." She continued down the row and he followed because—well, hell, what other choice did he have?

The next kennel contained a medium-sized black dog with a long, corded coat. The dog wagged when he saw them, and a pink tongue rolled out of his mouth.

"Is that a dog or a mop?"

Anna laughed. It was a delightful sound that almost made him smile. "That's Raszta. He's a Puli. His coat naturally forms dreadlocks, giving him the mop look."

Dreadlocks.

An image flashed in Zak's mind of a girl with dreads leaning over him, telling him he'd be okay, but it was there and gone before he could grasp it and bring the girl's face into focus.

He shook his head and let the dog sniff his hand. "Why is he in jail? He seems friendly."

"This isn't a jail, and he is very friendly... until dinner time. He came to us from a hoarding situation in Texas, where he used to fight around ninety other dogs to eat. He's food aggressive, but we're working on it. He'll make someone a good pet someday."

The final occupied kennel looked like a tornado had hit it. The bed was shredded, and cotton stuffing formed fluffy mounds like piles of snow. Kibble scattered the floor. The water bowl had been upturned and now sat in a small lake like a stainless steel island. The black and gold brindle dog in the middle of the chaos had startling yellow eyes that tweaked a thread of recognition in Zak's mind.

He stopped in front of the kennel and stared into those eyes. "I know this dog."

Anna nodded. "You met him once. The night of your accident, when Ash picked you up from the Mad Dog—"

"Ranger." He didn't know why the animal had stuck in his memory when everything else from that night was a blur. "He wanted to eat me."

"Well, don't take it personally. He wants to eat everyone and everything."

Ranger's radar dish ears twitched at his name, and he focused on Zak with the intensity of a heat-seeking missile. He got up and walked over to the door with the regal air of a king who had been waiting for his knight to return from battle. The series of exasperated huffs he gave sounded a lot like, *"About time you showed up!"*

"No teeth for me this time, mutt?" Zak knelt down, and his prosthetic knee thunked loudly on the concrete floor. Ranger cocked his head at the sound and stared at him with those freaky yellow eyes. He let the animal sniff his hand, then risked losing a finger by poking it through the bars and rubbing Ranger's black nose.

Anna glanced between the two of them. "Huh," she said after a long minute of silence.

Zak gazed up. "What?"

Her head tilted much like the dog's. "He rarely likes anyone but me."

"What's his story?"

Anna knelt beside him. "He was a military working dog, but his handler was killed in action, and he was badly injured. He came out of the experience with post-traumatic stress—"

"Dogs get PTSD?"

"Yep, same as people. Ranger was suddenly aggressive when he never was before, fearful of unexpected noises, hyper-vigilant, anxious. The military retired him and tried to adopt him out, but he was returned sixteen times for behavioral issues. They were going to euthanize him until we stepped in and rescued him."

"He's a beautiful dog. What breed is he? I never saw any like him in the Army. All the MWDs I crossed paths with were Malinois."

"He's a Dutch shepherd. Dutchies are cousins of the Mal and the German shepherd." She climbed to her feet and opened the kennel door. Ranger gave a slow wag of his plumed tail and bumped his head against her legs as she picked up his water dish. "I've been working with him every day, and he's made tremendous improvements. He'll never be a pet, but I have high hopes he might work again. Probably not in a war zone, but something like narcotics or cadaver detection isn't out of the question. He might even do well with search and rescue. He has the drive for it."

Ranger strutted over. He had a limp, too. Slight, but every time he put weight on his front left paw, his stride hitched. A long, mean-looking scar sliced down that front leg.

Zak reached out and slid his thumb over the scar. In return, Ranger bumped his head against Zak's metal leg.

"He has a plate and screws in there," Anna said. "He almost lost the leg."

A knot tightened in his throat, and he got to his feet as quickly as he was able. Which wasn't quick at all because of the damn knee locking up again. Shame burned across the back of his neck as he struggled. Fucking babies could stand up better than him.

He hated it.

He hated Anna for just standing there, watching him. He didn't want her help—that would be worse—but she could've at least looked away and offered a shred of dignity.

And he especially hated the dog with its PTSD and gimpy leg.

When he finally gained his feet, he didn't dare look at them. He didn't want to see their pity. "Are we done here?"

Anna said nothing for a beat. "Yes, we can be done for today. I'll see you tomorrow."

Anna's heart thundered in her ears as she watched Zak stride away, his back soldier straight. His long legs ate up the floor with only a slight limp, taking him farther away from her, both physically and mentally. She'd pushed him too far, too fast, and now he was building new walls like crazy while desperately patching up the ones he'd already constructed to keep them from crumbling.

The problem wasn't that he didn't care. It was always that he cared too much, and he didn't want to.

The dogs got to him, just as she'd hoped. She'd seen his fist clench when she told Matilda's tragic story. She'd seen his amusement at Raszta, the mop dog. And Ranger...

Ranger's story had hurt him. Cut too close. He'd seen himself in the dog, and he hadn't liked the reflection.

Ranger returned to her side and gave a questioning whine. *Where'd he go? I thought we were going to be partners.*

She patted his head. "Give him time, Range. Remember how you were at first? He hasn't made as much progress, but we're going to help him with that." As the bang of the front door echoed through the building, she looked up at the empty hallway again and smiled. "And now I know exactly how."

chapter
ten

BELLA FIRST NOTICED the man at the end of summer, one week before her mom left their campsite and never came back. The man stood on the cliff overlooking the beach where she and Poppy spent their afternoons hunting for good shells and building sandcastles. At first, she didn't think much about him. Lost Rocks State Park campground was packed with tourists, and it wasn't unusual for someone to stand on the cliff and take in the view of the impressive sea stacks jutting up from the crashing surf. She made note of his hoodie, but it was a windy day, especially up on the cliffs.

Poppy ran over and excitedly showed her a pure white shell with a perfect, unbroken curl. When she glanced back at the cliff a few minutes later, the man was gone.

The second time she saw him, Mom had been gone for a week.

It wasn't a big deal. Jessica often disappeared for days at a time, especially after a blow-up fight like they'd had. A week was abnormally long, but honestly, Bella didn't care. Life was easier without Jessica there, especially since she'd found a job trimming buds at a local pot farm. She could afford food and new clothes for her sister's first day of kindergarten.

Poppy was bright as a sunbeam in her yellow top and pink leggings, her blond ponytail swinging as Bella led her toward the school. The girl chattered excitedly about Mr. CJ, her cheerful and flamboyant new teacher, whom they had met last week, and didn't notice when they turned the corner and Bella's step faltered.

There was the man again.

The hair on the back of her neck stood on end. He wore the same hoodie as before—Army green with the brand's logo in black on the upper chest—but she still couldn't see his face or any other identifying features. She couldn't even tell his race. He was shadowed by his hood and the tree he stood under.

Was it Jake?

She gripped Poppy's hand a little tighter and hurried her through the school's front gate, which would be locked after drop-off. Poppy would be safe inside with Mr. CJ and her classmates. Of course, if Hoodie Man was Poppy's father—Jake Beckett, the sick pedophile hiding his twisted fantasies behind a detective's badge—then the school could release her to him. He had custody and parental rights. Bella didn't. She'd just have to make sure she was here right at the end of the school day to pick her up. She wouldn't give him the chance to steal her away.

When she stepped back out onto the street, the man was gone.

She shook off the chill of unease. It was nothing. He was just a parent dropping off his kid. He probably wasn't even the same man she'd seen on the cliff. His sweatshirt was a popular athletic brand found in every department store. Hundreds, if not thousands, of people likely owned the same one.

It wasn't Jake.

They were safe here in Steam Valley. Bella had a job and had even made some friends. Poppy had school. She'd make friends her own age and have stability for the first time in her young life. No way Poppy's asshole dad could find them here. Despite his widespread connections, he couldn't have tracked them all the way from Arizona. She was worrying for no reason. And she had to stop dwelling and get to work. Rainbow, her boss, was a nice woman but expected punctuality.

She would not let Mom's constant paranoia poison her mind and ruin the only good thing they'd had in a long time.

They *were* safe.

At least, she thought so...

Until later that night.

The sound of a car door startled Bella out of a sound sleep. She rolled over and checked the digital watch she'd bought at the local thrift store so she could get Poppy to school on time. The pale blue display showed 3 AM.

Her heart sank.

It was Mom finally coming home. Had to be. Nobody else would be at their campsite at this time of night, but why couldn't Jessica have just stayed away? Life was so much easier without her.

Bella scooted to the window and lifted the shade, but a dense gray fog draped the campsite and all she could see was the outline of a car, its headlights like beady yellow eyes in the gloom. Ghostly figures moved through the mist. Two? Three?

She squinted.

No, she only saw two. One was about the size and shape of Mom. The other was much bigger. A man.

Great. If Mom thought she was going to bring him in here for a fuck, she had to think again. Poppy had school in the morning and needed to sleep.

Bella could just barely hear their voices, muffled but... angry? Yes, that definitely sounded like anger, and more. Hatred. The man *hated* Mom. Even though she couldn't make out his words, the hatred seethed in his tone.

Oh, shit. This situation could go bad fast.

Nervous now, Bella edged off the bed, careful not to disturb Poppy, and double-checked that all the doors were locked.

Of course, Mom had a key, so if the man really wanted to get in, he could take it from her.

Not a comforting thought.

She could just start the van and drive off, leaving them here to deal with their shit without putting Poppy in danger. She'd been considering a move anyway and had her eye on an inland campsite away from the turbulent winter seas this area was known for. Or she could drive up to work. Rainbow had already said she could camp at the farm and that option saved her money, which she'd need if she wanted to find an apartment.

As the plans raced through her head, she pulled on her boots without tying them and gently woke her sister. "Pop, I need you to put your shoes and coat on." Just in case they had to run. "And then crawl into the front seat and buckle up for me, okay?"

"Why?" Poppy whined.

She didn't bother with a lie. Her brain was still sleep-dazed, and she wouldn't be able to come up with a fiction more compelling than the truth. "Because Mom's home and she brought someone I don't like."

Poppy's eyes widened. "Is he scary?"

"Maybe. Please, just get dressed and buckle up in case I have to get us out of here fast. Can you do that?"

She nodded solemnly.

Bella kissed her forehead. "There's my brave girl."

She watched Poppy pull on her rain jacket and boots and silently cursed their mother. No five-year-old kid should be so solemn or have to deal with these scary, adult things. She peeked under the blind again. There was a lot of movement, almost like the two were dancing together or—

Bang!

Bella's heart lunged into her throat as she drove for the driver's seat. The sound had been muffled by the fog, but there was no mistaking what it was: a gunshot. And she wasn't about to stick around to find out who had the gun.

"Stay down, Pop. Don't come up here! Just grab something and hang on."

She jabbed the key in the ignition and cranked it.

Nothing happened.

"No, no, no, no." She whispered the word over and over under her breath like a prayer. "Please start. Please."

She twisted the key again and got a faint revving sound in return. *Okay. Don't panic. It just needs time to warm up. Keep trying.*

Something heavy hit the side of the van, shaking the thing on its wheels.

Poppy screamed.

Bella choked back a sob and turned the key again with shaking hands.

The engine roared.

Choked.

Sputtered.

Died.

Someone threw open the sliding door, and fog curled inside the van like skeletal fingers. A man stood there, outlined by the other car's headlights.

He wore a green hoodie. And black leather gloves. And he was reaching for Poppy, who kicked at his outstretched hand in silent, wide-eyed terror.

"No!" Bella threw herself between them and clawed at his face with her ragged nails, but he was huge. So much bigger than she expected, with mounds of muscle like a bodybuilder.

He easily subdued her, twisting her arms behind her back and pulling her against his solid chest.

"Stop it," he hissed. "Please. I won't hurt you." He had an East Coast accent. Boston or New York; she couldn't tell. They all sounded the same to her.

And was he crying?

It didn't matter. She couldn't trust anything he did or said. Why else would he be doing this if he didn't want to hurt them?

She opened her mouth to scream. Maybe if she made enough noise, the Whelans next door would hear and—

He clamped a hand over her face, his beefy palm covering both her nose and mouth, and her scream died in her throat.

"I'm sorry," he said again and again as he dragged her from the van and locked Poppy in. Her boots came off and her heels touched something warm and wet on the ground.

She squeezed her eyes shut. Didn't want to look down. Couldn't.

But she had to.

Mom.

She lay face-down on the ground in a spreading pool of blood. The shawl she always wore—the one she'd stolen from a chintzy tourist trap shop in New Mexico—covered half her face. The other half of her face was... gone. Nothing but a mess of blood and bone and lumps of tissue.

Bile burned up Bella's throat and she clamped her teeth hard on the fleshy part of the man's hand. He released his grip on her mouth and she sucked down a lung-full of air.

"Poppy," she wheezed. "Please, don't let her see Mom like that. Please."

The man blinked and tears rolled down his dark face. "I'll take care of it," he said in a voice thick with emotion. He opened his car door and gently deposited her on the backseat, then locked her in and disappeared from view.

The car was still running.

She could run him over when he came back!

She dove into the driver's seat and swore when she realized why he'd felt safe leaving it on.

No key detected.

It was one of those push-button starts and he had the key with him. It wasn't going anywhere without him. She could unlock the door and run to the Whelan's campsite, but... no. The man would disappear with Poppy before she could get help. No way was she leaving her sister alone with him. She pounded the steering wheel with her fists in frustration, then realized—*duh, horn!* She could wake up the whole campground.

She balled her hand and raised it over the center of the wheel but froze when the man reappeared with a blanket and crouched over Mom's body. He rolled her onto it, then wrapped it around her lovingly, like he was swaddling a baby. He carried her to the back of the car. The truck popped open, and the car shifted at the additional weight. He hadn't thrown Mom in. He'd set her in there gently, carefully.

But... didn't he hate her? Bella was sure she'd heard the hatred in his voice earlier.

When he reappeared, he wore a jacket rather than the bloodstained hoodie. He opened the back door and placed a duffle bag on the seat.

"I'll get your sister now," he said roughly. "Stay here. Please."

"Okay." It was all so strange, and she didn't know how else to react. "Thank you. Poppy didn't need to see that."

He said nothing more, just shut the door and went to the van. Poppy was a ghost, her eyes showing too much white and glazed with the tears pouring down her cheeks. She didn't fight the man, and actually clung to his big shoulders. He picked up Bella's boots from the bloodstained ground on his way back to the car.

He handled Poppy as gently as he had Mom, tucking her into the backseat with another blanket before buckling her in.

Bella turned to study her sister. "Are you okay, Pop?"

The girl just curled in on herself and stuck her thumb in her mouth. That was a bad sign. Poppy had stopped sucking her thumb a long time ago.

Hoodie Man dropped her boots into the footwell under Poppy, then opened the driver's side door. "Move."

Bella climbed over the center console into the passenger seat. She tried the door handle but knew it would be locked. "Where are you taking us?"

He shoved the car into reverse. "Someplace safe."

chapter
eleven

ZAK HAD a firm idea of what group therapy would be—a mix of crunchy granola bohemian-types whining about how their chakras were out of whack; and middle-class, middle-aged men losing their hair as they went through mid-life crises; and overworked, under-appreciated housewives who used pills and wine to cope.

He dreaded it.

He didn't want to sit in a room and share his demons with people who didn't know what true suffering was, but he wanted his damn license back. Walking everywhere was getting old, and without wheels, he felt more trapped in this fucking town than usual.

If he could survive daily torture for over two weeks, these twice-weekly meetings should be easy. Maybe he could even skip the dog sessions. He'd have to double-check with his lawyer, but he didn't think it was part of his court-mandated therapy. Besides, he spent enough time with the animals as it was. The last three days of cleaning pee and poop and avoiding the dog with the yellow eyes and metal leg had been torture worse than he'd endured in Afghanistan. At least that kind of torture he'd been trained to withstand. This was hell. And, adding in group therapy, it was only going to get worse.

He arrived a half hour late.

Fuck walking, man. It always took longer than he expected, especially now with his half-metal leg. He used to do grueling ruck marches with fifty pounds on his back with little thought, but he no longer had the stamina for a short, hilly hike.

It was only when he saw Anna playing in the dog yard with Winston and Ranger that he remembered he was supposed to have been here an hour ago to help set up. So he was actually ninety minutes late. No doubt she'd have something to say about that.

Fuck.

Sucking in a fortifying breath, he pushed into the room Anna used for adoption and fundraiser events and found a group of five people seated in a circle of hard plastic chairs—three men and two women.

The older woman with the neat wire-framed glasses was Dr. Amelia Firestone. In another lifetime, she'd been his high school guidance counselor and had encouraged him to think about joining the Army since his grades sucked and he had no interest in college. Given how it ended up, he should hate her for it, but he couldn't even find that in the blessed fog of numbness he'd spent the morning curating with a bottle of Jameson.

Except for the new silver streaks in her black hair and a few more wrinkles around her gentle eyes, Dr. Firestone had barely changed.

The other woman had straight dark hair pulled back into a long ponytail and hard, dark eyes. He recognized her from around town but didn't know her name. She wasn't a local. She'd only appeared in the area about a year ago. A fluffy brown and white dog sat on her lap. It was wearing a plaid bowtie.

Seated to her left was a blond man in a USMC hoodie with a brown lab on the floor beside his chair. The dog wore one of those harnesses with a handle on the back and a vest that proclaimed her name was Zelda and she was a service animal at work.

Jesus. The man was blind.

The realization had a ball of dread rising in Zak's throat, and he slammed to a halt just inside the door. Every eye in the room turned toward him. Except for the blind man's.

And he remembered something Anna had said during his initial visit. *The only veteran treatment program in the county...*

These people were like him.

War survivors.

He wanted to back out of the room and run away as fast as his gimpy leg allowed.

"Zak," Dr. Firestone said warmly and waved him in. "Glad you could make it. Come in. Coffee and donuts over there." She indicated the table along one wall with her chin. "Help yourself and pull up a chair."

He couldn't move.

Dr. Firestone only smiled and turned back to the group. "Go on, Sawyer. You were telling us about your week?"

The blind man hesitated for a beat, and then his fingers flexed around the handle of his dog's harness. "So, uh, yeah. It's been a shitty week. Stuff I used to do all the time, the easy shit you don't think about, like making a coffee, is now this whole fucking process. I used sugar instead of coffee grounds yesterday and only noticed when I took a sip of hot sugar water. It's—" He broke off and seemed to search for the right word.

"Frustrating?" the female veteran suggested, sinking

deeper into her chair and wrapping her arms around the dog in the bowtie. The little creature licked her cheek.

"Infuriating," another man said. He was a big guy with full tattoo sleeves, and his voice broke the immobility spell keeping Zak's boots glued to the floor.

Shocked, he strode forward. "Donovan?"

Again, everyone looked at him.

Donovan Scott glanced over his shoulder, gave his trademark smirk and a two-finger salute. "Hey, Zak."

"What the fuck are you doing here?"

"Zak," Dr. Firestone said, her voice somehow both firm and gentle. "We never question each other's motives for therapy, okay?"

"No, I didn't mean—" He stared down at the man who had once been one of his best friends. He, Ash, and Donovan raised so much hell together as kids the townspeople had called them The Terrible Trio. "I thought you were still overseas."

Donovan tapped the rope of scar tissue on the side of his face. "Got blown up. Head trauma. They discharged me over a year ago."

He'd been back in town a whole year, and Zak hadn't known. "Man, I'm—I'm sorry."

"Is what it is."

The bland statement ignited the simmering well of resentment inside him like a match to gasoline. "What kind of Buddhist bullshit is that? 'It is what it is?' You're just accepting it?"

Donovan's smirk faded, and he pushed out of his chair. He was as tall as Zak, and they were almost nose-to-nose. "What, you think the way you've been handling your shit is better? You think I didn't try it that way, too?" He waved an arm at the group. "We've all been there, done that, got the T-shirts and scars. I almost killed myself and ended up here, and now I don't think about swallowing a bullet every day. So, yeah, I'm accepting it. I can't change my scrambled, fucked-up brain."

"And I'll never see again," the blind man, Sawyer, added.

The third man in the room, who still hadn't said a word, thumped his hand on the arm of his chair to get everyone's attention. His neck was scarred extensively, like something with big teeth had tried to rip out his windpipe. Donovan glanced over, and the man grunted, making a lot of movements with his hands.

"Pierce says he'll never speak again. And *you* can't grow another leg," Donovan finished. "It is what it fucking is, and now we have to learn to live with it."

"We're all here because we're dealing with something," the woman said. Unlike the men, she didn't explain what her *something* was. Nor did she give her name. She continued hugging the dog like a shield and eyed him with suspicion over its ridiculously fluffy ears. "You're not special."

Dr. Firestone rose from her seat and picked up a folded chair from the stack next to the coffee and donuts. She opened the chair and placed it between her and Pierce. "Here. Take a seat, Zak."

He stayed where he was. He didn't want to know more about these people or their problems and absolutely didn't want to tell them about his own. He didn't care. Couldn't. Because caring about others fucking hurt. Caring had cost him his leg, his life... his sanity.

Dr. Firestone left the chair empty and returned to hers. "I'm sorry you've been struggling, Sawyer," she said, picking up the conversational ball that had dropped when Zak interrupted. "When we're born with sight, it becomes second nature. We rely on it for everything, but take it for granted, thinking we'll always have it. It's the same with hearing or speaking or"—she nodded toward Zak— "a missing limb. We don't realize how much of our identity is tied into that piece until it's gone."

Sawyer exhaled hard. "I remember how hard it was at first. I fought against re-learning how to live."

Zak shifted uncomfortably on his feet. This guy was blind, and wasn't even looking in his direction, so why did it feel like he was staring right into his soul?

"Everything felt impossible," Sawyer continued. "Like my doctors and family were asking me to climb Everest with no equipment or training. Sometimes it still feels that way. I miss being able to chill out and watch TV. I miss video games and going to see a new movie with friends. I can listen to it, but it's not the same." He gave a self-deprecating laugh. "And not that I have friends anymore. I pushed them all away because I hated them for still having what I didn't."

Pierce grunted and made a bunch of insistent hand movements.

Donovan translated. "What about us?"

Sawyer's lips twitched. "You assholes don't count."

A ripple of laughter went through the group. Even the woman cracked a small smile from behind the shield of her tiny dog.

Dr. Firestone gave them the moment of levity, then shifted in her seat to face Sawyer again. "And how have things been since you received Zelda?"

"She's magnificent." He bent over to stroke a hand over the dog. Her tail thumped on the floor. "I don't know how I survived without her. She's given me a freedom I didn't think I'd ever have again. We went for a hike yesterday." A grin split his face. "She took me on an eight-mile hike."

"Tell us about it."

Sawyer exhaled hard, and when he spoke again, his voice was thick with emotion. "You know, before, I was always in the mountains. Camping, hiking, rock climbing. It was like a church for me." He wiggled his fingers at his temple. "It quieted my mind like nothing else. And after, I couldn't—" He broke off.

"We're not talking about that," Dr. Firestone said gently. "We're talking about yesterday. How did it feel?"

He nodded and swallowed hard. "I couldn't see the scenery, but it didn't matter. I thought it would, but it didn't. It felt so fucking good to be out there again, to have a bag on my back and a path under my boots. I didn't realize how much I missed it until we were up on the mountain, and I could hear the waves crashing below, the birds calling out to each other, the trees rustling. I felt the wind on my face and breathed it in. It smelled faintly like smoke from the fires down south, but I didn't care because I finally found it again—that quiet in my mind. Zelda gave that back to me."

"I'm so happy for you," Dr. Firestone said, and it sounded like she truly meant the words. "How are the nightmares?"

Goddammit. Zak didn't want to hear about anyone else's nightmares. He had enough of his own, thank you very much. He eyed the door. Would it violate his probation if he bolted?

Probably.

Fuck.

Sawyer's smile faded. "Yeah, um..." He cleared his throat. "Uh, you know, good nights and bad nights."

"We all know that roller coaster," Donovan said, and a ripple of agreement went through the room.

"But Zelda helps there, too," Sawyer added. "She wakes me up when it's a bad one. She's not even trained for that. I think she just worries about me."

"I wish I had a Zelda," the woman said and hugged the little dog closer. He snuggled in under her chin even though he apparently didn't belong to her.

Dr. Firestone shifted in her seat to face the woman. "How are you, Veronica? You've been quiet lately."

Veronica's gaze flicked to Zak, then cut away. "I don't want to talk."

"Okay. That's okay." Dr. Firestone's gaze followed. "How about you, Zak? Can you tell us a bit about yourself?"

He tried to say, "hell, no," but his throat closed up as every gaze pinned him down. He couldn't breathe, couldn't hear beyond the thunder of his heartbeat in his ears.

He couldn't do this.

Violation or not, he had to leave.

Right now.

chapter
twelve

ANNA SAW Zak leave the barn like his ass was on fire then stagger to a halt in the middle of the driveway. She looked down at Ranger and Winston, who were laying in the grass at her feet, tongues out, taking a break from their game of fetch.

"Looks like group therapy went well. Honestly, he lasted longer than I expected. That has to be a promising sign, right?"

Winston continued to pant happily.

Ranged grunted and stretched out on his side.

Out in the driveway, Zak glanced around like he was lost, then bent double and placed his hands on his thighs, gasping as if he'd finished a marathon and couldn't catch his breath. Her smile faded.

Uh-oh. That was a panic attack. She'd had enough of them to know the signs, even from a distance.

She jogged across the field with the dogs racing at her heels. When she climbed over the fence, Winston skidded to a halt and sat down to stare at her through the wire with wounded eyes. Ranger didn't slow. He bounced off the side of the barn and took a flying leap, his sleek body stretched out long. He cleared the fence with feet to spare.

Okay, then. A six-foot fence was not a deterrent for her Houdini dog. Good to know.

She winced when he landed and his bad front leg gave out, but he recovered quickly, limping only slightly as he streaked toward Zak.

Ugh, those two were a pair. The dog, like the man, always pushed boundaries. Neither of them wanted to accept their limitations.

She made it to Zak's side steps behind the dog. His face was startlingly red, like he was choking. She rubbed his back. "It's a panic attack. Breathe through it."

He shook his head.

"Yes, you can. Follow my breathing. In and out. Nice and slow."

He sucked in a sharp breath and let it out in a ragged exhale.

"There you go." She took him by the arm and guided him over to the house. They were at the porch before he thought to shake her off.

"I'm fine."

He still didn't look it. Now he was pale, and his hand shook as he rubbed it down his face.

"Sit down," she said. "I'll get you something to drink. Water?"

He collapsed onto the porch steps. "Whiskey?"

"Water it is." She went inside and filled a stainless steel bottle for him and a bowl for Ranger. Before heading back out, she snagged a banana from the fruit basket. He needed food, and he'd always liked bananas when they were younger. She had to assume he still did.

At the screen door, she stopped short, and her heart squeezed. Ranger sat next to Zak, chin resting on his knee. He was miles away, staring off into the distance, but he still stroked a hand absently over Ranger's head.

There was no therapy in the world like the love of a dog.

She purposely shifted her weight so the floorboards under her creaked before she opened the door. She didn't want to startle him.

Zak glanced back and accepted the water and banana without a word. He drank down half of the bottle in one breath, then peeled the fruit and ate on autopilot.

She set the bowl down for Ranger, but it was ignored. For some reason, the dog was enamored with this man. Maybe Zak reminded him of his former handler. Or maybe it was simply because he could sense they were kindred spirts.

Not that she could blame Ranger. She'd been enamored with the same man at one time, but he'd broken her heart.

And so much more.

As much as she wanted to help him—*needed* to help him for the sake of her family's land and the future of her rescue—she couldn't risk falling for him again.

She sat on the step beside him and together they watched the rest of the group leave one by one. Dr. Firestone was last, and as usual, she came over to the house to drop off the key for the community room. Alfie, her therapy trained Papillon, looked snazzy in his plaid bowtie as he rode in her oversized tote, his fluffy ears flapping in the breeze.

Zak wouldn't look at the doctor as she made small talk for a few minutes, and she let him get away with it. She was a good doctor, but sometimes she was too soft. Zak needed a firmer hand.

Anna waited until Dr. Firestone's car was headed down the driveway, then she scowled at him. "Coward."

His spine snapped straight. "What?"

"You heard me."

"Do you have any *idea* what I've done? What I'm capable of?" His voice was deadly calm, and his eyes went hard and flat. She imagined it was the face his enemies had seen in war before he ended them. A shiver raced down her spine, but she wasn't about to back down. Someone had to call him out on his bullshit if the therapist wouldn't.

"Oh, believe me, I know. I've heard all the stories. You were a badass black ops soldier. A war hero. And that's amazing. Truly. Most men couldn't do the things you have, but right now, at this moment?" She pointed at the cloud of dust kicked up by the doctor's car. "You acted like a coward. You couldn't even look that sweet woman in the eyes and say hello."

He wanted to protest. She could see it in the defiant line of his jaw and the tick of muscle as he ground his molars. He removed Ranger's head from his knee and pushed to his feet. "I'm leaving."

She let him get a few steps away before calling, "Aren't you forgetting something?"

He stiffened like he expected an attack but didn't turn back. "What?"

"Since you were late and missed set-up for the therapy group, you still owe me your community service hours for today."

Zak swore, spitting every colorful combination of four-letter words he knew. This woman called him a coward, and now she wanted him to spend the next several hours cleaning up dog shit at her beck and call.

He'd killed men for less.

And she thought he was a hero. Ha. She had no idea the man he was.

Fists balled, jaw clenched so tightly he was giving himself a headache, he faced her again. "What do you need me to do?" He had to squeeze the question out between his teeth.

She grinned. She was obviously enjoying herself. "Give me a piece of your clothing."

He wasn't even going to ask. He peeled off his overshirt, thankful there was enough of a bite in the air today that he'd layered up. He tossed it to her.

She caught it and looped a hand through Ranger's collar before throwing a ragged rope toy in his direction. He wasn't expecting it and nearly dropped the thing. Ranger made happy dog noises and his entire backside wagged.

Anna laughed and patted his side. "Patience, pup."

Zak held up the toy. "What the hell am I supposed to do with this?"

"Go hide and give him that toy when he finds you." She nodded toward the woods. "Whistle when you've found a place. And don't half-ass it. Find a good, well-concealed spot so Ranger can practice his tracking skills. I don't want him getting rusty in his retirement."

"Great," he muttered and stuffed the rope in his back pocket. "Now she has me playing hide and seek with a dog."

"Would you rather pick up poop?" she called. "Because that's still an option."

He gave her the finger over his shoulder and plunged into the woods.

A few feet in, the world morphed into an alien place where everything was impossibly green. The color dripped and drizzled around him, clinging to the thick redwood trunks in blankets of moss and carpeting the ground in feathery clusters of ferns. All-encompassing, the green muffled all other noise while it whispered and beckoned and seduced you deeper into its cool grasp.

It was... nice. Soothing. Peaceful.

He *enjoyed* being out here.

How could he have forgotten that about himself?

He followed a narrow winding path for a while until he came to a bridge he remembered from his childhood. He and Ash used to spend summer days here, jumping off the bridge into the creek below. The water was shallow now from an extremely dry summer, but by winter it would be a bubbling, chattering stream of ice cold snow melt from the mountaintop.

Okay, then. If Anna wanted a challenge for the dog, he'd give her a challenge. He put two fingers in his mouth and gave a sharp whistle that cut the church-like silence of the forest, then he hopped over the railing and landed ankle deep in the creek. His boots were waterproof, so he wasn't worried about his prosthesis rusting, but he cursed when the knee locked up again. He slammed a fist against it a couple of times.

Hell, maybe it'd be a good thing if it rusted. Then the VA might get off their asses and actually process his request for a new one.

Nah, probably not. He'd just end up with a locked knee and a rusted foot. Hence, the waterproof boots—and he was still too much of a soldier to skimp on caring for his boots. Footwear could make or break a mission. He'd seen it happen plenty of times.

He slogged downstream until the creek deepened and forced him onto the bank. He took stock of his location and decided to circle back and head up the mountain. By the time he found a hiding place in a craggy spot on a steep grade, he was sweating and out of breath.

Holy shit. If he didn't stop sucking in air like an asthmatic, Ranger would hear him before scenting him. He forced himself to take slow, deliberate breaths until he stopped gasping. Man, he'd really let himself go. That uphill climb should've been easy. A few years ago, he could've done it with a hundred extra pounds on his back.

Hell, he *had* done it. He'd all but carried a terror-stricken Tehani up a hill like this—with a fucking sprained ankle, no less—while Taliban fighters chased them.

"This is Zak. I need an exfil now."

Static replied, but he thought he heard a voice mingling with the white noise.

"I repeat, this is Sergeant Zak Hendricks. I've been made. Get me the fuck outta here."

"Zak?"

He jolted at the voice and lashed out at the hand on his shoulder.

"It's okay," Anna whispered. "It's just me. And Ranger's here, too. You gave him a good run, but he found you. Can he have his toy?"

Numb, he grabbed the toy from his back pocket and offered it to the dog. Ranger took it but spat it out and nudged his cheek with a wet nose.

"I'm okay, mutt." He didn't sound okay, though. Even to his own ears, his voice was thin and reedy.

Anna sat on the small bolder that shielded his hiding spot. "Where were you just now?"

He exhaled hard and dropped his head into his hands. "Afghanistan."

"Do you want to talk about it?"

"Fuck, no." He used the rock outcropping to pull himself upright, and once again, he had to pound on his stupid mechanical knee to get it to straighten correctly. He held out a hand for the rope toy. "Let's go again."

"Are you sure?"

He spotted the rope on the ground where Ranger had dropped it and scooped it up. Without answering, he strode away to find another hiding spot.

HE DIDN'T FREEZE up again. But, Anna noted, he always stayed under the green canopy of the redwoods and didn't venture up the mountain again, where the terrain could be mistaken for another set of mountains on the other side of the planet.

By the third round, when Ranger found him in a hollowed-out tree, he even seemed to enjoy the training exercise. He threw the rope toy and made a sound that almost passed for a laugh when Ranger pounced on it.

He ducked out of the tree and brushed himself off. "Take off your clothes."

She gave a startled laugh. "Excuse me?"

His eyes didn't quite sparkle with mischief like they used to, but there was a spark of amusement there. He smirked. "Get your mind out of my pants."

"*You're* the one telling *me* to undress."

"Because it's your turn to hide. I wanna see how he works. Show me how to give him the scent."

A thrill shot through her belly, and not only because he was joking about undressing. He was finally showing an interest in *something* besides drinking himself to death. More than once today, she'd caught glimpses of the old Zak, the kid she'd once loved to distraction.

He was coming back to life.

So she spent the next half hour coaching Zak on how to give Ranger a scent and how to handle him while he searched. Once she was satisfied, she pulled off the bandana keeping her hair out of her face and offered it to Zak.

"Sure," he said to the dog with an exaggerated eye roll. "I give her a shirt, and she gives me a lousy bandana."

"Play your cards right, soldier, and you might get to see more." Her face flamed as she darted away to find a hiding spot, and she was so glad he couldn't see her tomato-red cheeks.

Holy shit. Why did she say that?

She paused at the creek to splash her face with the cool water and let her scent pool, then zig-zagged over it a few times before finding the old hunting blind between two trees. She used to play out here all the time when she was a girl, pretending it was her castle and she was the lost princess waiting for her knight to rescue her.

Little did Young Anna know, *she* would be doing the rescuing more often than not. And she actually preferred it that way.

The blind let her watch Zak and Ranger's progress. They worked together flawlessly, as if they'd been training for years. As if she needed any more proof that the two of them were soul mates. Now she just had to convince them of it.

Nose to the ground, Ranger zig-zagged over the creek, never missing a beat. Zak struggled to navigate the uneven ground because of his prosthetic. There had to be a way to get him a new one that didn't lock up all the time. She'd have to ask Dr. Firestone about it.

Ranger came straight toward her and circled the base of her trees several times, then sat down. He didn't alert. The poor thing just looked confused.

"What's wrong, mutt?" Zak asked. "Did you lose the scent?" He pulled her bandana out and let Ranger sniff it again.

Ranger huffed, circled the trees, and again sat down in confusion.

Zak ran a hand through his hair and scanned the forest. "Aw, fuck. Did she lose us?"

Anna stifled a giggle behind her hand.

And her phone signaled a text.

Both man and dog looked up.

"Real cute," Zak said dryly.

Ranger popped to his feet, his entire body wiggling as she tossed him his rope. She climbed down and checked her phone's screen. "Looks like we're done practicing for today. Winston and I have a real call out."

"You mean a search and rescue call?" Zak fell into step next to her as she hurried back toward the house. "Can I come?"

"I don't know how much of a rescue it will be," she warned. "It sounds like a recovery mission."

"The dead don't bother me."

She shot him a doubtful glance.

"It's the memories that get to me," he said softly and tapped his temple. "The nightmares."

God, she wanted to hug him.

And because of that, she picked up her pace. "If you're coming with, you gotta keep up."

Anna was amazing.

When they got to the Lost Rocks State Park camp-grounds, both she and Winston, the goofy golden, slid into work mode. Ash was already there with a handful of his deputies, cordoning off the beach, the campgrounds, and the parking lot.

"What do we know?" she asked her brother as he lifted the police tape to let her through.

Ash scowled at Zak and dropped the tape before he could duck under. He just glared back and ripped through the plastic.

Ash growled. "What's he doing here?"

"He's helping." Anna clapped her hands in front of her twin's face. "Focus. We're running on a limited watch. What do we know?"

Ash drew a breath and waved for them to follow him across the campgrounds to a beat-up camper van from the seventies. It was pale blue with a faded yellow peace sign decal on the side. Something about the van was familiar, but Zak couldn't place where he'd seen it before.

"We have a missing family," Ash said, all cop again. "A mother and two girls—one a teenager and the other elementary age—were reported missing this morning by their neighbors in the campsite next door."

"Tourists?" Zak asked.

"We don't think so. The mother may be a trimmigrant working at one of the pot farms up the mountain. She's been seen hanging around The Palace a lot, and the campground manager said the family's been here all summer." He nodded toward a massive RV at the next campsite. A family of picture-perfect blonds stood in front of it, talking to one of the deputies. "That's the Whelans from Utah—Tad, Jenna, and their daughters. They called in the report. They were packing up to head home today and found this." He motioned them over to the camper van.

Zak skidded to a halt. That smell. Even before he saw the red stains, he knew what he'd find.

Blood. A lot of it. The ground was soaked, and the van's partially open panel door was splatter-painted.

"The Whelans saw the older girl and her mother in a fight yesterday just after lunch," Ash said. "The mother slapped her around before taking off. It was bad, but it doesn't account for all this blood. Mr. Whelan said he heard a banging sound, like a gunshot, around 3 AM, but when he looked out the window, he saw nothing out of the ordinary."

"That's a lot of blood," Zak said. "Someone was killed here."

Ash nodded. "So now you see why I think this is probably a recovery."

"If there are bodies here somewhere, Winston will find them." Anna stroked her dog's head. "What are the victims' names?"

"Hang on. Let me double-check. I didn't take the initial report." Ash grabbed a tattered notebook from his jeans pocket and thumbed through the pages. "Okay, yeah. The mother is Jessica Lowe, thirty-five years old, Caucasian, approximately five foot six, one-twenty, blond and blue. The kids are Bella, sixteen, mixed race, five-five, skinny—one-ten at most—with dyed blond hair and brown eyes. And Poppy, five, around three and a half feet tall and thirty pounds, blond and blue."

Poppy.

The name reverberated through Zak's mind like a plucked guitar string. Why did he recognize it? He searched his memory and only found the faint echo of a phrase repeated again and again.

They'll take Poppy from me.

Anna touched his arm, drawing him out of his head and back to the here and now.

"Did you see something?" she asked.

Shit. How long had he been staring blankly into the woods? He knew and appreciated what she was attempting to do—she was afraid he'd regressed into memory again like on the mountainside and didn't want him to embarrass himself in front of Ash.

He shook his head. "No. Just... that name rings a bell. Poppy?"

"That's the five-year-old," Ash said, suspicion dripping from his tone. "Why would you know *her* name?"

He glanced over at the man who had once been more like a brother to him than his actual blooded brother. "C'mon. Hate me, fine, but at least give me the courtesy of pretending you know me better than that. I would never hurt a child."

"Ash, apologize," Anna demanded.

Ash exhaled hard. "Sorry. I wasn't implying anything." He ran a hand over his face. "I'm tired and punchy."

"Ask me," Zak said, "this is a marked improvement from your usual point and grunt."

Ash clenched his teeth. "You just love pushing my buttons, don't you, Hendricks?"

"You have so many fun ones to push."

"Oh, both of you, grow up." Anna elbowed her brother, then shoved a finger in his face. "Don't make me regret bringing you."

He held up his hands in surrender and backed up a step. "I'm a ghost. Won't even know I'm here."

"Yeah, right." She drew a breath through her nose, let it out in a huff, and returned her attention to Ash. "Do we have a description of what the girls were last wearing?"

Ash nodded and consulted his notebook again. "The

Whelans weren't sure about the mother other than the long shawl she always wore. They described it as multi-colored, with a southwest Native American design on the back. Bella was last seen wearing a gray hooded sweatshirt under an over-sized red flannel, black jeans, and combat boots. Poppy was in purple leggings, a pink long-sleeve T-shirt featuring the Disney character Stitch, and flower rain boots. She also has a pink puffer jacket with a flower design on the front pockets."

"Okay." She patted Winston's side. "Ready to work, buddy? Let's find these girls."

Zak stepped out of the way and watched from the outskirts of the crime scene as Anna and her dog worked. They moved together in a well-rehearsed dance born from a mix of intense training and instinct—just like soldiers. They were a team.

Damn, he missed being part of a team.

Ash stepped up beside him, arms crossed, jaw set. "I know what you're thinking."

Temper flared hot along the back of his neck. "The fuck you do."

"The old rule still applies."

"What, the dumb-ass Bro Code?" He scoffed. "It was stupid then, and we're not bros anymore."

"She's off limits."

"That's her decision." Why was he even arguing about it? He had no interest in sex with Anna or anyone else. He was too busy battling the demons in his head and trying to survive each day, but he wasn't about to say that to Ash.

Better to just remove himself from this conversation.

He turned away, but Ash caught his arm in a bruising grip. "She doesn't need you fucking up her life again."

Zak met the man's gaze, surprised to see it burning with hatred. "Again?"

"Sheriff?" a deputy called out from the neighboring

campsite.

Ash released him and walked away.

chapter
fourteen

THE SEARCH TURNED UP NOTHING.

No sign of the mom or kids.

Winston kept catching a scent, but then he would endlessly circle the campsite. She could only assume it was because all the blood confused him. They wanted him to find decay, but it was all over that campsite.

So much blood.

Luckily, Zak held up better than she'd expected him to. She'd had reservations about taking him after the incident while playing with Ranger.

"The dead don't bother me. It's the memories that get to me."

What memories? What had happened to him over there?

She angled her rearview mirror to see the backseat. Winston hated to disappoint, and whenever he couldn't complete the job he'd been tasked to do, he got depressed and moped. When the search was finally called off because of rain and darkness, Zak climbed into the backseat to soothe him. She figured they both needed the reassurance and didn't say a word about it as she slid behind the wheel.

Now they were both asleep. Zak's head tipped back against

the headrest, and Winston's big square head was on his lap. His hand was still buried in Winston's wet fur.

She hated to disturb them, but they were nearly to Zak's. His cabin was tucked away on Bluff Road, its cedar shake siding grayed by decades of ocean storms. His parents had built the small two-bed, one-bath home when they first moved here in the late 70s with their newborn daughter Jamila, and it still had "The Hendricks Family" carved into a plank over the carport. When Zak came along, the cabin became too small for the growing family. When Taj arrived two years later, they moved to a bigger house in town but still kept the cabin as a vacation rental until Zak returned from Afghanistan and needed a place to live. Now it was worth at least ten times what they'd paid to build it.

Why wasn't Monarch Development trying to bully the Hendrickses into selling? It was prime oceanfront property that bordered the Rawlings land they wanted so badly.

Actually, they probably had made an offer, Anna realized as she pulled into the driveway. And she wouldn't be surprised if Paksima Hendricks had told them to shove their offensively minuscule check where the sun doesn't shine and go take a flying leap off the bluffs. Zak's mother, the current high school principal, wasn't afraid to tell people exactly what she thought.

Anna parked behind Zak's truck, which sat unused in the carport with a boot on the back tire. No doubt Ash's handiwork. As far as she knew, that wasn't standard practice for a DUI. Her brother probably put the boot on as a precaution to keep Zak from driving without a license because as much as he complained about Zak, and as much as they butted heads, she knew he cared.

Zak had so many people who cared about him and he didn't even realize it.

She shifted in her seat to look at him. Winston was awake

now and gave a slow tail wag when he saw her watching. His eyes seemed to say, *I'm sorry I disappointed you.*

She reached back to rub his soft muzzle. "You're a good boy, Winny. The best. You could never, ever disappoint me."

Zak jolted awake with a gasp and looked around like he didn't know where he was.

"Hey, you're okay," she said in the same gentle voice she used for the scared and abused dogs she rescued. She set a hand on his knee. "You're home."

He focused on her like she was a lifeboat in a turbulent sea. After a second, the fog of sleepy confusion cleared, and he groaned softly, scrubbing his hands over his face. "Sorry. Must've fallen asleep."

"Yep. You were snoring." He wasn't, but the appalled look on his face was worth the white lie.

"I don't snore."

"Like a foghorn."

"I don't—" He noticed her smirk and shook his head. "You're a brat."

"You used to like that about me." Oh, shit. There went her mouth, saying things before her brain told it not to.

"I still do," he said so quietly she almost didn't hear him over her racing thoughts.

Something changed between them at that moment. The air felt charged, like electricity danced over every surface and if she touched him again, they'd create sparks. But it wasn't an uncomfortable sensation. Instead, with the rain pattering on the roof and windshield, the dark vehicle felt safe and cozy, and... *intimate*. She could tell him anything right now, all her secrets...

Damn, this was dangerous.

She should turn on the overhead light and cut through the intimacy with the harsh yellow glow, but then he'd see the blush heating her cheeks. Before she could decide, he spoke again.

"Do you... want... to come in?"

Yes.

She closed her eyes and imagined it. His hands on her body, finding all the secret places it seemed only he knew about. The places that made her gasp and quake and melt. She'd had other lovers since him—some of them quite good— but none had ever made her want so thoroughly or come so hard as Zak Hendricks. She'd accepted long ago that no man she invited into her bed would ever live up.

So, yes, she desperately wanted to go into that cabin and find out if sex with him was as good as she remembered. After the stress of the fruitless search, she needed the release.

Except.

The halting way he'd asked was a huge, waving red flag. He wasn't ready for a relationship, even if it was just a one-night stand. He had to re-learn how to take care of himself first, and he had a long way to go.

She opened her eyes and found him watching her intently in the darkness. She smiled, hoping to soften the blow. "I should go home."

He said nothing for several heartbeats, then nodded and shoved open the car's door. He was pissed. She could see it in the tight line of his shoulders and his stiff movements as he climbed out of the vehicle.

"Zak, wait. It's not..." Too late, she realized she couldn't take that sentence any further without revealing too much, so she let it trail off.

"Not what?"

She sucked in a sharp breath. "A good idea."

He ignored her and leaned in to give Winston a final pat on the head. "You're a good dog," he said, then shut the door.

She rolled down the passenger window. "I'll see you tomorrow."

He stopped short, and his shoulders rose and fell with the deep breath he took. When he turned back, rain streamed down the expressionless mask of his face. "The cadaver stuff. Could Ranger do that?"

She stared at him, thrown by the abrupt subject change. "Uh... well, I don't see why not. He's already familiar with tracking live humans. We'd simply have to train him to recognize the scent of decomposition, too."

"I want to do it. I want to train him."

Her heart grew wings and fluttered wildly around her chest, but she kept the joy off her face. "I think he'd love that."

"Okay." He wiped the rain from his face and continued on to his front door. "Tomorrow, then."

chapter
fifteen

"GOOD MORNING, EVERYONE." Dr. Firestone set her tote beside her chair and the little black, brown, and white dog poked his head out, his wing-like ears all but flapping. Today, his bowtie was black with shiny gold swirls all over it. He jumped out of the bag and patrolled around the room, intently sniffing everybody like he was looking for something.

That tiny animal couldn't possibly be the same species as Ranger and Winston.

It looked more like a stuffed toy than a dog, Zak decided as it came over to sniff the boot of his prosthesis. He shook his foot. It barked—a surprisingly robust sound with only a bit of the squeak Zak had expected.

He smirked down at it. "What's your name, little dude?" He only realized he'd spoken out loud when conversations ground to a halt and everyone looked at him.

"That's Alfie," Dr. Firestone said, breaking the silence. "He's an emotional support animal and therapy dog."

Alfie sniffed his boot again, then sat. The dog's big ears flipped back as he tilted his head up to give the biggest puppy eyes Zak had ever seen.

"And," she added with a smile, "it looks like he's chosen you today."

Zak scowled at her. "What?"

"He's psychic," Sawyer explained and felt around for his chair before he sat. He folded up his cane and set a hand on Zelda as she settled in beside him. "He always knows who needs the most support."

"Jesus. Psychic dogs?" He shook his head and went back to doctoring his coffee. Strong with lots of sugar—he'd need both the caffeine rush and sugar high to get through this damn meeting. He hadn't slept a wink last night, but for once, it wasn't memories of Afghanistan keeping him awake. It was memories of Anna—her hands on his body, her lips on his, the silk of her red hair fanned out over his thighs as she—

Damn.

He took a big drink of the too-hot coffee and realized everyone was staring at him expectantly. The dog was still at his feet. "What do you want?"

Alfie barked and stood up, dancing in circles on his hind legs.

"He's an emotional support dog." Sawyer grinned. "Obviously, he wants to support you."

"I don't need support."

"Then why are you here?"

"Court order."

Sawyer nodded. "Ah, yes. We've all been there."

"Several times," Donovan said and scooped up a muffin from the tray. "Hey, Daredevil. Catch." Then he fast-balled the muffin at Sawyer's face.

Even more shocking, the blind man lifted a hand and caught it easily before it hit in square in the nose.

Zak nearly dropped his coffee. He glanced back and forth between them, his mouth working soundlessly.

Donovan smirked and grabbed another muffin, taking a bite. "Didn't see that coming, did ya?"

"I did," Sawyer said.

"What. The. *Fuck*?" Zak finally managed. He pointed an accusing finger at Sawyer, heat rising up the back of his neck. "You're not blind. What was all that shit you said last time about—"

"No, I am."

Pissed, Zak picked up another muffin and threw it. Again, Sawyer caught it. And, this time, he threw it back. Zak did not catch it. It bounced off his chest and rolled across the floor.

"They're messing with you," Veronica muttered. She was already curled up in her seat, legs drawn up under her oversized hoodie. "Sawyer can see movement."

"Aw, way to ruin our fun," Sawyer said. "I wanted to see how pissed he got at me."

"Okay, that's enough." Dr. Firestone took her seat. "This is supposed to be a safe space, so we won't be hazing every new guy."

Everyone except Veronica groaned. Even silent Pierce made a bunch of hand movements that looked like he was saying a lot of unflattering things.

Dr. Firestone ignored them and patted the empty chair next to her.

Zak walked over and sat before he realized what he was doing. Alfie followed and danced on his hide legs again, his front paws pressed together like he was praying.

Okay, fine. Alfie was ridiculously cute. Who could resist those Dumbo ears?

With an exasperated exhale, Zak caved and scooped the dog up. Alfie turned circles on his lap, then curled into a soft, warm ball. And, dammit, it was comforting. His blood pressure, which had been in dangerous territory all morning, instantly dropped.

A psychic dog.

Who'da thunk it?

Dr. Firestone nodded with satisfaction. "All right, since everyone's here, let's begin. Sawyer, do you want to start by telling Zak about your condition?"

"Yeah, sure. It's called Statokinetic dissociation, or Riddoch phenomenon," he explained and grinned. "Like Vin Diesel in *Pitch Black*."

"Nah, not the same." Donovan took his seat between Sawyer and Pierce. "Riddick could see in the dark. The way you sense things, you're more like Daredevil."

"Whatever." He waved a dismissive hand in the air. "Point is, I'm legally blind, but I can still see movement. Like that steam rising off your coffee."

Zak looked down at his cup. Sure enough, thin wisps of steam danced over it. "Holy shit. How?"

"I was on patrol in Afghanistan right before they pulled us out. I was days from going home and caught a sniper's bullet right here." He tapped the back of his head. "My helmet stopped most of it, but it fragmented on impact, and a piece got through to damage my occipital lobe. There's nothing wrong with my eyes; they can see fine. My brain just doesn't know it. Or, to be more precise, it can't process the information it gets from my eyes like it's supposed to. So, I see nothing until something moves, and my brain remembers that—oh, hey, we *can* see—for just an instant. When the movement stops, I'm blind again."

"Brain trauma really fucks with you," Donovan muttered. "I can't remember shit anymore. This morning I stood in front of my bathroom mirror for a good ten minutes, my face all lathered up, my razor in my hand—and I couldn't remember how to shave. It's so simple, and I couldn't figure it out. So, I washed my face off and came here to tell you guys about it and, fuck me, if I didn't suddenly remember just now."

"Brain trauma can feel vicious," Dr. Firestone said. "Cruel, even, because everything that makes you *you* is stored in your brain, so when it's damaged, it can feel like you've lost yourself."

"I sure as fuck don't feel like myself anymore," Donovan said. "I don't know who I am now."

"Me, either. But, hey, I'm starting to find out." Sawyer smiled down at his dog with his heart in his sightless eyes. "And at least I can see Zelda's tail when it wags."

At her name, her tail thunked on the floor.

"Like that. Or when I take her out to the dog yard here, release her from her harness, and let her zoom. I can watch her run and, for a minute, feel normal."

"I get it. Yesterday, I—" Zak bit down hard on his tongue to stop himself from saying more. Jesus. It was like his mouth had a mind of its own lately.

"Go on," Dr. Firestone prompted. "What did you do yesterday?"

Fuck. He glanced toward the door, but he had a sleeping dog on his lap. He couldn't make a clean escape this time.

Trapped.

Donovan leaned back in his chair and smirked, crossing his tattooed arms. "C'mon, Zak. We showed you ours. Time to strip down and show the goods."

Veronica rolled her eyes. "You're disgusting."

He grinned at her, but there was an edge of mean to it. "You don't have a vote because we still haven't heard your tale of woe."

"Oh, fuck you, Van."

"Name the time and place, sweetheart."

"Donovan," Dr. Firestone said, her voice like a whip. "That's enough."

"Yeah, you're right. That *is* enough." He shot to his feet and kicked his chair across the room. "We can sit here and talk everything to death, but it won't change the fact my brain is Swiss cheese. So, fuck this. I'm outta here." He punched the wall on his way out, leaving a hole in the drywall by the door.

Veronica withered into her chair and pulled up her hood.

Sawyer set a comforting hand on Zelda's big brown head.

Pierce stared hard at the wall across from him.

Nobody said anything for several long beats, then Dr. Firestone inhaled hard and exhaled a slow, deliberate breath. Then she smiled, but it was strained around the edges. "Tell us what you did yesterday, Zak."

He opened his mouth to say, "hell, no," but then glanced over at the hole in the wall and shut it again without uttering a sound. He stroked his fingers over Alfie's soft fur. The dog stretched out his little paws and arched his back, then repositioned and fell promptly to sleep.

Zak scanned the expectant faces around him and decided it was easier to focus on the dog on his lap. He rubbed Alfie's Dumbo ears between his fingers. "Yesterday, I played hide and seek in the woods with an incredible dog, and I laughed with a beautiful woman, and I felt... normal. For the first time since I lost my leg, I felt almost whole again, but then I went home and drank half a bottle of Jameson and didn't sleep because I knew the nightmares were right there waiting for me." He looked up at Dr. Firestone. "I want to feel normal again. Will coming here help me?"

She nodded toward the rest of the group. "Ask them."

Zak looked at Veronica since she was seated right beside the doctor. "Is it helping you?"

She lifted a shoulder. "I don't leave my house, but I'm here, aren't I? That has to tell you something."

Pierce clapped to get everyone's attention, then his hands moved in a series of gestures Zak couldn't decipher. He'd have to learn sign language if he was going to be hanging around the guy.

"He says therapy works," Sawyer translated.

"Wait, you can see what he's saying?" Zak asked.

"His hands are moving."

Okay, wow. He still couldn't wrap his head around that. It must be a difficult way to live, caught in limbo between sight and blindness. "And what do you think?"

Sawyer stayed quiet for a moment. "We are broken people carrying our busted pieces as best we can. Some days—like today for Donovan—are brutal reminders of everything you've lost, but he'll come back next time. We all return because in this room when one of us inevitably drops some or all of those pieces, we know the rest of us are right here to pick them up and help glue them back on. So, yeah, it does work, but it's not easy. If you're going to be part of our group, we need you all in with us." He paused and looked toward Zak's seat. "Are you in, or are you just here to fulfill the court order?"

Even though Zak wasn't moving, and Sawyer couldn't possibly see him, it felt like the guy was staring into his soul. He finished his coffee and released a shaking breath. "I don't know."

chapter
sixteen

ZAK STAYED in the community room long after the therapy session ended. He told himself it was because he was supposed to tidy up, but even after he folded all the chairs, took the leftover muffins to the staff at the vet clinic next door, and cleaned and primed the coffee maker for next time, he still lingered. Despite what he told himself, he knew exactly why he was reluctant to leave. He'd dreaded seeing Anna again since the awkwardness of last night.

But he couldn't stay here forever if he wanted to train Ranger as a cadaver dog.

Dammit, he *was* a coward.

He found Anna in the kitchenette of C-Wing. She wore surgical gloves and had an array of glass vials spread out on the counter in front of her. There was also gauze, small canvas bags with Velcro enclosures, and a short length of PVC pipe with holes drilled in it. If he didn't know her better, he'd think she was making a bomb. "What are you doing?"

"Hey, you're just in time. I'm preparing for our first training exercise." She tilted her head, indicating he should come in and shut the door. "We're teaching Ranger to recognize the scent of death today. You'll want some gloves."

He glanced around and spotted the open box of surgical gloves beside the sink. He grabbed a pair, then realized they were too small and set them aside. Found a box of larges under the sink and slipped the gloves on as he returned to her side.

He picked up one of the glass vials. "Pseudo-Corpse? Does it really smell like a dead body?"

She smirked. "Give it a sniff."

How bad could it be? Shrugging, he opened the cap and inhaled, then immediately regretted it as bile surged up the back of his throat. He coughed and started to close the vial, but she laughed and held out a hand.

"Give it here."

He coughed again and passed it to her. "That's... potent."

"You're not supposed to stick your nose in it, dumbass." She used a dropper to put a little of the scent on a gauze pad, then closed the vial and placed the gauze in one of the canvas bags.

"Is that enough?"

"More than. Remember, a dog's sense of smell is up to one hundred thousand times more sensitive than ours." She passed the canvas bag under his nose. "Can *you* still smell it?"

He gagged and waved it away. "I think the scent is burned into my nostrils."

She laughed again, and he found his own lips twitching with amusement. He enjoyed making her laugh. He liked the fizzy champagne feeling her laugh caused in his blood. "What do we do next?"

"Well, here. Why don't you do it? You need to learn." She handed him the canvas bag. "These bags are used to train dogs on the scent of drugs, but it works for decay, too. It allows scent to escape but keeps the dog from getting to what's inside. That's especially important when we start using actual human material."

That gave him pause. "We'll use real bodies?"

"No, that's illegal. But I do have a stash of dirt I've collected from underneath bodies—with permission. The scent soaks into the ground and makes a fabulous training aid. And all of my volunteers know if they have any teeth pulled, I want them. One of my volunteers even donated her placenta after she gave birth, which was so amazing of her. It's all in that freezer over there."

He eyed the chest freezer in the corner of the room. And here he'd thought that was for dog food or something. "I'm never eating here again."

She smacked his arm. "It's important to train with more than just the Pseudo-Corpse because bodies release all kinds of different aromas as they decay. We want to expose our dogs to as many of those scents as possible." She slid the length of PVC pipe toward him. "I go the extra step of putting the bag in this. It's probably unnecessary with the narcotics bags, but this is how I was trained to do it."

He dutifully stuffed the bag inside the pipe, then capped the ends.

"All right." She stripped off her gloves. "Let's go out into the yard and hide it."

Zak removed his gloves and followed her out into the dog yard. "How long will the training take?"

"It takes anywhere from eighteen months to two years to earn a cadaver dog certification, but Ranger already knows how to track a living person. It's what he did in the military, so that might give us an advantage. Or it might hinder us. It could be a simple matter of teaching him we also want him to look for this new scent, or we might have to retrain him completely. We'll see how he responds today. He's a smart boy. I know he'll catch on fast."

On the way outside, Anna picked up a stack of plastic barrels and placed them in a line in the center of the yard. She then went to a storage shed and grabbed another one.

"This is the 'hot' barrel," she said as she returned. "We always put the pipe in the same one and store it separately from the others, so the dogs aren't confused by lingering trace odors." She set it in the line and motioned for him to place the pipe inside. "Now, since Ranger is trained to track humans, you'll want to go through and touch all the other barrels, too, or else he could just track your scent to the right one. We want him to start to recognize the cadaver and ignore your living scent."

Zak touched each of the barrels.

"Okay, good. Go get him and bring him out on a leash. You'll walk him past the barrels, and as soon as he shows any interest in the cadaver scent, give him his blue rope as a reward."

Ranger knew something new and fun was happening when Zak attached the leash. His radar dish ears twitched, and his body quivered with excitement.

Zak took a moment to give him a quick scratch and pep-talk. "You got this, mutt. I know you do."

But Ranger didn't seem all that interested in the scent at first. He walked up and down the line of barrels, completely ignoring the one with the pipe in it.

"It's okay," Anna called. "Take him to them one by one. When you get to the cadaver, have him sniff, then give him his toy and praise him."

After that, the lightbulb clicked on in his smart doggie brain and he went right to the barrel with the cadaver scent. They ran the exercise repeatedly, moving the barrel with each round, and he nailed it every time. They also tried it off-leash with the barrels scattered across the yard rather than in a line, and once again, he zeroed right in on the cadaver scent.

"Good dog!" Zak clapped and hooted as Ranger did a victory lap with his toy, strutting like a show horse around the yard.

Anna nodded. "Very good dog. I knew he'd catch on fast. Tomorrow, we'll work on adding a command, so think of the word or phrase you want to use. 'Track' is his live-search command, so you could go with 'find,' 'look,' or even 'search.' Just stay away from 'dead' or 'stiff' or anything like that. It has to be sensitive enough to use in front of victims' relatives because they will often work with you to find their loved ones. A lot of trainers use 'find the napoo.'"

"Napoo?"

She shrugged. "It means dead. Some say it's a Native American word, but I think it's actually slang from World War I, a corruption of the French phrase *il n'y a plus*, meaning 'there is no more.'"

"I'm not using napoo."

"That's fine. Use whatever works for you and Ranger. Whatever command you decide, he'll pick it up fast."

Ranger tossed his toy into the air and caught it before whipping it around.

Zak grinned. "Look at him. He's proud of himself."

"He should be. And you should be proud of yourself, too. You're a natural dog handler."

"No, it's not me. It's all him. He's so fucking smart." He felt her gaze on him and glanced over. She watched him with soft eyes and a sweet smile. "What?"

"I haven't seen you grin this much since we were kids." She touched his cheek, brushing her thumb over his heavily stubbled jaw. "It looks good on you."

He shifted toward her, and just like the first time he'd kissed her all those years ago, he didn't think about it. He leaned down and pressed his lips to hers. Unlike the first time, she didn't react right away. She let him kiss her but held back. Just when he started to wonder if he'd made a mistake, she took fistfuls of his shirt, surged up onto her toes, and met the seeking thrust of his tongue with her own. She tasted as sweet as he remembered, and an uncomfortable prickly feeling raced over his skin as she deepened the kiss. It felt like when a leg went to sleep and all the blood rushed back too fast, except it was his entire body waking up, not just one limb. His heart suddenly felt too big for his chest, like he was the Grinch and it had tripled in size.

No.

He couldn't breathe.

It fucking hurt.

He didn't want all these feelings. He wanted to be numb again and heard the siren song of the whiskey he had waiting at home. It beckoned to him, promising a night of peaceful oblivion.

He broke the kiss.

She looked so beautiful with her face turned toward his, her cheeks flushed, her lips rosy. All the more reason he should leave. She was beautiful, inside and out. He was a grotesque, half-dead creature that would suck the life out of her if he stayed around.

He backed up a step and thrust Ranger's leash at her. "I need to go."

She blinked. "Wait, what? Where?"

"Anywhere but here."

"Zak." Her voice broke on his name as he turned away. "Please don't go home and drink. You're doing so good."

chapter
seventeen

ZAK STEWED on her words the entire two-mile walk back to his cabin. Who was she to tell him what he could and couldn't do? If he wanted a fucking drink, he'd take a fucking drink, and she couldn't stop him.

As soon as he stepped into his house, he grabbed the bottle waiting on the kitchen counter and twisted off the cap. Except when he raised it to his lips, he stopped before a drop touched his tongue. The smell turned his stomach.

If you're going to be part of our group, we need you all in with us.

Are you in...?

Zak threw the bottle in the sink, watched the drain glug it down, and panicked. What the fuck was he doing? He needed the alcohol to sleep. He grabbed the bottle and took several long, deep swallows.

We are broken people carrying our busted pieces as best we can...

He leaned over the sink, head pounding. His chest burned from the whiskey and still felt too tight for his heart and lungs to function properly.

Jesus, why was breathing so hard? He'd been doing it his

entire life, but now it took all his focus just to suck in air and push it out.

In.

Out.

In.

Out.

The tightness eased.

In.

His lungs opened.

Out.

He turned around and slid down the cabinets until his ass hit the floor, then pulled off his prosthesis and rubbed the stump. It ached.

Was it any wonder Anna had rejected him last night? And when he kissed her today, she should've shoved him away, but she was too nice. She glowed with warmth and kindness. She was perfect and no red-blooded, heterosexual male in his right mind would turn her down. She had her pick, so why would she choose a man with one leg and demons riding his back?

Jesus.

He didn't know how long he sat there drinking. Long enough that his butt went numb, and the cold of the kitchen tiles seeped into his bones. Long enough that he finished the half bottle. He got another from the pantry across his narrow kitchen by using his prosthesis as a hook to open the door and roll the bottle within grabbing distance.

He drank and watched the shadows of evening lengthen and blacken into night. He watched the night fade to gray. Sometime in the early morning hours, when his second bottle was light and his head was still buzzing with dark thoughts, he wondered what was the point of surviving Afghanistan? He should've died over there. At least then he would've been a hero and not a useless, broken burden.

He could die now.

The thought sliced through him with a knife's edge, but instead of pain, he experienced a euphoric rush of relief. He'd gone about it all wrong out on the highway six weeks ago, trying to make it look like an accident. If he wanted it done, he had to man up and use a gun. Better chance of success that way.

He took another drink of Jameson and used the counter to pull himself up, not bothering to put his leg back on. His gun was in a wall safe behind his couch. It'd only take a few hops to cross the distance and then it would be over.

Something dropped out of his pocket and clunked on the floor. His phone. He picked it up. The screen showed a call was in progress, and he squinted at the ticking numbers. It had been going for a while.

He raised the phone to his ear. "Hello?"

"Zak!" The relief in the deep voice on the other end was tangible. "Jesus fucking Christ. Are you okay?"

"Whoz dis?"

"It's Greer."

Greer Wilde. His commanding officer in the black ops death squad he'd been a part of, and the man who was responsible for his rescue. It had been a fully deniable op, so when he was captured, he'd known no help was coming—but Greer had gone against orders and hired mercenaries to find him. He owed the man his life. For what little it was worth.

"You don't remember calling me?" Greer asked, worry edging out the relief.

Now that he mentioned it, the fuzzy memory of reaching for the phone bobbed to the surface of his alcohol-flooded brain. "Yeah. Kinda."

"We've been on the phone for hours. You were talking about suicide and how I should've left you in Afghanistan, then went silent—" Emotion broke in his voice. "Zak, man, you need help."

"I don't need—"

"Yeah, I thought the same thing, but I was wrong. Everything got better when I finally reached out to my family, my loved ones. I know you have people who care about you. Lean on them until you're strong enough to stand by yourself."

"I've done enough leaning, thanks." Though he was leaning now, staring into the sink. Where was the water coming from? The faucet wasn't on.

Oh. Right. His face. He was leaking.

A woman's voice murmured in the background, and he cursed as he swiped at his eyes. Greer was married now. His life was good, all candy hearts and sunshine bubbles. He no longer spent his nights wasting away on booze and bad memories.

"Sorry, shouldn't've called."

"Yes, you should've," Greer said sharply. "You can always call me. Night or day, drunk or sober. You hear me, Hendricks? *Always.*"

"Sir, yes, sir," Zak muttered and grabbed a bottle of Jameson on the counter, only to find it empty. He threw it in the sink, where it shattered.

"All right, I'm coming out there. You shouldn't be alone."

"No, I'm juss drunk. I'm fine. Really. Won't do anything stupid. Promise."

Greer said nothing for a second. "Drink some water. Go to bed. I'll call later and you better answer or I'm getting on the next flight out."

"Yeah, okay. Later." He stuffed the phone into his pocket and looked toward the wall safe.

Fuck it.

He wanted the gun.

He was done with this shit.

chapter
eighteen

ON MONDAY, Zak didn't show up for his community service.

Anna told herself not to worry. After the kiss, it shouldn't surprise her he'd ghosted. This was perfectly on-brand for him: run away and stay away. Isn't that exactly what he'd done fifteen years ago? He'd run from her arms into the arms of the Army.

And look where that got him.

Dammit, she was worried. He shouldn't be alone with his memories.

She debated whether she should go check on him all morning. Not that she could get away, even if she wanted to. Sasha's receptionist had called in sick, so she'd volunteered to answer phones for the vet clinic, and they never stopped ringing. She barely had time to take a breath between calls.

But Ash was coming over for lunch today. She could ask him to do a quick welfare check on his way...

Yeah, no. Sending him to Zak's would be like throwing a match into a jug of gasoline. *Boom.*

Zak was fine. Or, at least, as fine as he usually was. Which, let's be honest, wasn't fine at all.

Someone cleared their throat, and Anna realized the phones had stopped ringing. She gazed up at her best friend. Sasha LeBlanc was a beautiful woman with dark hair and eyes, more curves than a mountain road, and one of those husky, femme fatale voices that made even the blandest of statements sound sexy—but she didn't see her own beauty. She was always too worried about her weight, constantly on one fad diet or another. She was currently on a juice cleanse and the concoction in the tumbler she carried looked like pureed grass.

"You're biting your nails," she said with a knowing smirk, and took a drink of the green stuff. She winced but tried to cover it with another determined sip.

Anna looked at her ragged nails. "Dammit. They were actually growing for once, too." She eyed the tumbler. "Sash, please just eat a sandwich."

"No. It's good." Her face at the third sip said otherwise, and she set the drink down on the reception desk. "Why don't you drive over to his house and check on him?"

Was she that obvious?

"No, it's fine. He's fine." She busied herself with straightening the reception desk. Instead of pinning the phone messages to Sasha's cork board in the treatment room as they came in, she'd let all the call back slips pile up. "Sorry I didn't get these back to you sooner. There are some semi-urgent questions in there and at least one med refill that needs to be done today and—"

Sasha stilled her hands. "It's okay. Go check on Zak."

"He's probably just drunk or hungover or both. You need my help here. I don't know how Mary-Lisa does this every day and makes it look easy. I'll be hearing that phone in my sleep."

"Because she's a superhero, and we're lost without her." Sasha took off her lab coat and hung it on a hook behind the desk. "But we're closed for lunch now, and my schedule is light this afternoon. My techs and I can handle the phones, so *go*. I'm a big believer in following your instincts, and yours are —" She broke off.

"Are what?" Anna glanced up and grinned when she saw why Sasha had stopped talking.

Ash stepped into the office in full uniform. He usually wore jeans and a button-up to work unless he had something official to do. Today was an official kind of day, and as a woman, she could appreciate how handsome he looked in the wide-brimmed felt hat, khaki shirt, and dark green tie, pants, and jacket with his badge on the breast and the Lost County Sheriff's Department patch on the arm.

But, as his sister, she was obligated to tease him. "Oh, look, Sash. I didn't realize Smokey the Bear had an appointment today."

"Ha ha," Ash said, deadpan, and took off his hat. "Hey, Sasha."

"Hi," she replied so faintly it was barely a breath of sound. Her face flushed bright red, and she snapped up her drink, backing toward the swinging door to the treatment room. "I, uh... should... lunch. I mean, duh, it's lunchtime. I should go... eat... er, drink... lunch." She spun and whacked her shoulder on the doorjamb as she pushed through. With how fair-skinned she was, she'd probably have a hell of a bruise.

Anna winced in sympathy and looked at her brother. "She likes you."

He stared at the door Sasha had disappeared through, his lips compressed into a thin line. "I know. Her, and every other single woman in the county."

"It was that Most Eligible Bachelor article in the paper when you were elected."

He growled. "I wish I'd never agreed to that publicity stunt. Now, are we gonna eat or what?"

She grabbed her jacket from the back of her chair and circled the reception desk. "Well, if you weren't a bachelor anymore, it wouldn't be a problem. So, when are you going to ask Sasha out?"

"I'm not."

"Why?" She faced off with her brother, arms crossed. "She's gorgeous, sweet, and intelligent. You can have an actual conversation with her—once you get past her shyness. She's leagues better than the women you usually go for. And you both love animals. You're perfect for each other."

He put his hat back on and held the door open for her. "I don't date. I—"

"Yeah, yeah." She puffed up her chest and deepened her voice, swaggering like a cowboy from an old western as she walked past him. "'I don't date. I fuck.'"

He winced. "I've never said that."

"You might as well."

"I don't date"—he enunciated each word— "because I don't have time for a relationship."

"Correction: you don't date because one-night stands with air-headed tourists are easier than taking the time for a relationship."

A low sound of annoyance rumbled in his throat. "Why are you like this?"

She gave her sweetest smile and looped her arm through his as they walked across the driveway toward the house. "Aw, you'd be lost without me."

"I swear, AJ, sometimes..."

"Sometimes you wonder how you got so lucky to have me as your twin. I know. I get it. I'm awesome."

"You're a brat."

And that made her think of Zak again. All the worry she'd been able to push away for the last few minutes came flooding back. Her smile faded.

"What's wrong?" A frown creased Ash's forehead. "I

didn't actually hurt your feelings, did I? You know I never mean—"

She waved it off. "No, it's not you."

Now his frown turned dark. "Zak." A statement, not a question.

She worried her lip with her teeth. "You didn't... receive any calls about him over the weekend?"

"No. Should I have?"

"I don't know. He didn't show up today."

"That violates his probation."

She stepped in front of him and pressed a hand against his chest to stop him from rushing over there. "Don't. Please, Ash. It's not a violation. It's... something else, and I'll handle it after lunch."

His eyes narrowed, but when he opened his mouth to argue, his phone rang. He grabbed it and looked at the screen. "Sorry. This is probably about that missing family."

"Of course. Go ahead and answer."

She shamelessly listened in while he took the call, but he said little. It was just a lot of typical Ash grunting and an abrupt "yes, keep him there," followed by, "okay, I'm on my way."

"Catch a break in the case?" she asked when he hung up.

"No. We're still at a dead end, but the father just arrived. He's a detective down in Arizona and has been searching for his ex-girlfriend and the kids for years. He was awarded primary custody of the younger girl—his biological child— and temporary emergency custody of the older girl, but the mother took off with them instead of complying."

"Oh my God."

"Yeah, it's a mess. I gotta go."

"Let me know if you need Winston again."

"It'll probably come to that. My gut tells me they're dead, and we need to be looking for bodies. This new information, coupled with the fight the neighbors witnessed between the mother and older daughter, makes me think we're dealing with a murder-suicide situation." For a moment, his strong shoulders sagged like he carried the weight of the world. "And now I have to go tell a father that."

"Hey." She caught his hand before he turned away and stepped into his arms, hugging him tightly. "You got this."

He exhaled a long, ragged breath. "Thank you. I *would* be lost without you." He squeezed her back hard and kissed her forehead before releasing her. "Since we're not having lunch, you might as well go check on Zak now. I can tell you're worried."

"You are, too."

"Yes," he admitted grudgingly. "Fuck him, but I am. He was like a brother once."

"I know."

He went over to his truck. "Keep me updated?"

"Yep. You, too." She blew him a kiss. "Love ya, big bro."

"Ditto, little sis." He cracked a smile, slid behind the wheel and pointed the Tahoe toward town.

Anna waited until his truck pulled onto the road at the bottom of the driveway, then turned to retrieve her car keys from the house. She only made it a couple of steps before Oliver Lawrence came running out of the barn.

"Anna!"

She stopped and waited for him to catch up. He was a local kid who wanted to be a vet and worked half days as part of a new work-study program the high school was trying out with their seniors. Sweet, a little nerdy and prone to theatrics, but a hard worker. And he adored the dogs.

"Everything okay, Ollie?"

He shook his head but couldn't form words between his wheezing breaths.

She sighed and patted down his coat pockets. "Where's your inhaler?"

He fumbled it out of an inside pocket and depressed the button, sucking the medicine in. When he caught his breath, he huffed out two words that froze her blood: "It's... Ranger."

"What about him?"

"He was there when I fed him before school this morning, and I'm sure I locked his kennel but when I went in to clean just now, he—he wasn't—and I thought maybe you had him but here you are and he's not—"

"Whoa, wait. Slow down and take a breath before you give yourself another asthma attack."

He stopped and sucked in several deep, stuttering breaths.

"Okay, good. Now, slowly, what's wrong with Ranger?"

"He's gone!"

chapter
nineteen

BANG BANG BANG BANG!

Zak peeled his eyes open and realized the incessant pounding wasn't only in his head.

The door.

Someone was at the door.

And... someone was in his bed with him?

With a lot of hair.

And a tail.

And dog breath.

What. The. Actual. Fuck?

He bolted upright, and his stomach revolted. He had to clamp his jaw shut and swallow hard to keep everything in place. When he was sure he wouldn't vomit all over himself, he carefully shifted to look at the brindle dog stretched out on his back, paws in the air. "Ranger?"

Ranger's plumed tail lazily beat the bed, but he didn't open his eyes.

No.

Wait.

This wasn't right. The dog couldn't be here. Was this a

hallucination? Was he seeing things now? Because that would just be the cherry on the shit sundae that was his life.

Zak poked Ranger's belly, and he felt real enough. Nope, not a hallucination. Somehow, the dog was actually in his bed.

"Jesus, mutt. Get down!"

Ranger huffed, then twisted his body in a spine-defying way and melted off the bed, front paws first. He paused, gave a yoga-like stretch and a yawn, then walked forward until his back paws hit the floor. He shook, his collar clinking as it swung back and forth, then sat and stared unblinkingly at Zak with excited golden eyes.

So, what are we gonna do today?

Zak stared back at him, uncomprehending. "I—wha—you —" He scrubbed his hand down his face. "How'd you get here?"

The pounding started on the door again, and he suddenly knew exactly who was on the other side.

Anna.

He scowled at the dog. "You're about to get me in trouble, aren't you?" Grabbing his phone from the nightstand, he ignored the notifications about missed calls from Greer Wilde, his parents, and his siblings, and checked the time. "*More* trouble. Fuck."

So maybe it wasn't Anna at his door, but Ash coming to throw his ass in jail for violating his probation.

The world rippled around him as he stumbled out of bed. He had to grab the nightstand to steady himself.

Damn, when had he stopped drinking last night?

He hadn't even reached the hangover stage yet, though he didn't really feel drunk, either. Just dizzy and faintly nauseous.

And where the hell was his leg?

He hopped over to the dusty arm crutches propped in the corner of his bedroom. He hadn't used them since he first learned to walk again, but he was sober enough to realize one-footing his drunk ass to the door was asking for disaster. As he crossed through the living room, he spotted the leg hooked in the pantry's handle and vaguely remembered using it to get another bottle of whiskey from his stash.

Ranger trailed after him, wagging the whole time.

The shadow in the door's frosted window was too petite to be Ash. Thank God for small, red-headed miracles.

Anna called his name, her voice filled with worry. Her fist was raised to pound again when he pulled open the door.

Sunlight blasted his retinas, and he squeezed his eyes shut. "What?"

Shit. That wasn't what he'd meant to say.

Her eyes widened as her gaze skimmed his body, and he realized he was only in his boxers. She could see everything— every scar on his skin, his bare stump. Nothing was left to her imagination.

Shame burned through him. "Yeah, it's ugly. I'm not the handsome kid you knew anymore. What do you want?"

Her eyes met his, and he *hated* the pity he saw there.

"You didn't show up," she said without condemnation, and that pissed him off even more. She should be mad. She should be furious.

"So why are you here instead of your brother? I violated my probation. Shouldn't he be slapping handcuffs on me right about now?"

"Because I told him I'd handle it. Is Ranger—" Her gaze dropped to the dog, and she smiled. "I thought so."

"I don't know how he got here." But even as he spoke, the memory bobbed up through the haze of alcohol.

He'd had his gun in hand and was trying to grab the box of bullets from the back corner of the wall safe when he heard a scratching at the door. Ranger had worked the latch and let himself in and at the sight of him, Zak had broken. He'd dropped the gun, grabbed the dog, and cried.

If Ranger had arrived a few minutes later, it would've been too late.

He set his hand on the dog's head and all of his anger evaporated in a profound wave of gratitude. "I want to adopt him."

Anna's eyes widened. "Uh... what?"

He'd surprised her. Hell, he'd surprised himself. He'd never planned on having a dog. He could barely take care of himself. But Greer was right, and he shouldn't be alone. Ranger had been there for him when he'd most needed a friend.

"I want to adopt him," he said with more confidence.

Anna stared over his shoulder at the disaster area he'd been living in, and embarrassment heated the back of his neck. She started to shake her head, the "no" already forming on her lips, but then she stopped and looked at him. Really looked. It was impossible for her to know what he'd nearly done to himself last night, but in that moment, she must have seen it in him. Her eyes teared up, and she dropped her gaze to Ranger, who pressed closer to his one leg.

She knelt in front of the dog and rubbed his radar dish ear. "You knew he needed you."

"Yeah, he knew," Zak answered for Ranger, his voice cracking. "He stayed in bed beside me, and I didn't dream. I slept, Anna. For the first time in years, I slept."

She exhaled softly. "Okay." Standing, she met his gaze. "I can't let you adopt him until I'm satisfied he will be safe and happy here, but we can do a trial foster-type situation. If it goes well, and you complete your community service and quit drinking and stay out of trouble, then we'll talk about adoption." Her nose wrinkled as she shouldered by him. "And we need to clean your house."

She eyed the leg still hanging from his pantry door but said nothing about it and opened the fridge.

It was barren.

"What do you eat?" She shut the door and scanned the rows and rows of empty liquor bottles lined up on the counter. "Never mind." She started gathering the bottles.

He reached for them. "I can—"

She easily sidestepped him and dumped the bottles into the empty recycling bin. "No, you're going to shower off the liquor-sweat. You stink." She pulled the prosthetic leg free of the pantry and handed it to him. "I'll get started cleaning up, and then we'll go to the grocery store and the farm supply." With that, she left him standing there, holding his leg.

"Wait, why the farm store?"

"Because if you want to keep Ranger, he'll need supplies—food, bowls, treats, toys, a bed. And, speaking of food, we'll get food while we're out because I'm hungry and I'm not eating here until this entire kitchen is scrubbed with bleach." She opened the cabinet under the sink and found a bucket, scrubber, rubber gloves, and a bottle of bleach that he hadn't even known about. He'd never looked under the sink before.

"Well, why are you just standing there? We have a lot to do." Anna snapped on the gloves and started filling the bucket. "Move it, soldier."

chapter
twenty

THEY WENT to the farm store first, and Zak cursed when he saw the total. Ranger had been glued to his side since they left the house and now sat by his boot, ears pinned back, watching the cashier swipe the new bed and toys with curiosity.

He scowled down at the dog as he pulled out his credit card. "You're gonna break me, mutt."

Ranger's ears popped up. He stood and wagged his whole body.

Zak's scowl faded into a faint smirk of amusement, and he reached down to scratch the dog under the chin.

Anna's heart swelled as she watched them. This was good. This was healing—for the both of them. She'd been working with Ranger for months now, and the improvement in him just since he met Zak and started cadaver training was astounding. She'd taken the wrong approach with his rehabilitation— he'd only needed a person and a purpose.

And Zak needed this dog.

God, she hoped this arrangement worked out.

While they loaded the supplies into her Kia, Anna's stomach rumbled loud enough that Zak heard it.

He side-eyed her. "Hungry?"

She slid into the driver's seat and pretended her face wasn't turning bright red. "I was supposed to have lunch with Ash, but he was called away on the missing family case."

"Anything new there?"

She shook her head. "At least, nothing he'd tell me. Those poor kids. I don't think this will end happily."

"Cases like this rarely do." When her stomach grumbled again, he nodded out the windshield toward Main Street. "Isn't there a new cafe in town?"

"Hot Shots." Which was owned and operated by Monarch Development, who bought out the building's previous owner, kicked out the mom and pop shop there, and installed their own franchise. If anyone from corporate saw her, they might think she'd reconsidered their offer after their most recent thinly veiled threat.

She made a face. "I'd rather not go there. What about The Grove?"

He narrowed his eyes at her. She was testing him, and he was fully aware of it. The Grove was a staple in Steam Valley, having been in business for over fifty years. It was where all the locals hung out, and they would undoubtedly run into people they knew.

His jaw tightened, but he shrugged like it was no big deal. "Fine with me."

The bar and grill was an unassuming log building nestled in a grove of young redwoods, from which it got its name—it used to be The Groovy Grove, but the owners changed the name when the word groovy fell out of style in the eighties. The parking lot was packed with the dinner rush and people clustered at tables on the wraparound porch. Propane heaters helped ward off the evening chill.

Anna kept an eye on Zak as she circled the lot, looking for an open spot. He'd gone silent and stared at the diner like it would explode at any second and tear a hole in the universe.

Dammit. Maybe this was too much. He needed a gentle push, not a shove off a cliff.

She pulled into a parking spot and shut off the engine. "You don't have to do this."

Ranger pushed between the seats to nuzzle him, and he patted the dog's nose. "I'm okay, buddy. We'll be back soon." He shoved open the door. "Let's get this over with."

As they crossed the parking lot, a man she didn't recognize approached them, hand outstretched. He was a tall, muscular man with neatly cut blond hair and hard hazel eyes. There was an air of danger about him that had the hair rising on her arms in warning.

Zak flinched and panic flashed in his eyes before he shoved her behind him, putting himself between her and the stranger. "Stop right there."

God. He was terrified, and yet his first instinct was still to protect her.

The man stopped several feet away and held up his hands. He was carrying a stack of flyers and nothing more, but Zak still didn't relax.

"Sorry," the man said. "I didn't mean to startle you. I'm just—" He pulled a paper from the stack and held it out. "Have you seen my daughters?"

Zak stared at the man for a beat, then slowly reached for the flyer. Emotion flickered over his face as he looked at the missing poster—there and gone in a flash. The man wouldn't have seen it because he didn't know Zak, but to her, it was like a neon sign. He recognized the photos.

She stepped out from behind the shield of his body. "You're the father of the missing girls?"

The man nodded and held out his free hand. "Jake Beckett."

"Anna Rawlings. And this is Zak."

"Rawlings?" he asked as he shook her hand. "Like the sheriff?"

"My brother. He'll find your daughters."

His lips tightened. "He's not doing enough. They're in danger. He should have his entire department out there looking for them."

Annoyance snapped through her. He was upset. She got that. But it didn't give him the right to disparage her brother when Ash had been working his ass off since the night he received the call. She opened her mouth to tell him exactly that, but Zak put a hand on her arm, stopping her.

"We haven't seen the girls," he said.

Jake eyed them. "Call that number on the flyer if you do."

"Sure thing." Zak folded the flyer, slid it into his pocket, and put a possessive hand on the small of her back, steering her toward the restaurant.

She waited until they were well out of earshot. "But you *have* seen those girls. You recognized them."

He shook his head and glanced back at Jake. "Not now."

She also looked back, saw the man was still standing right where they'd left him, staring after them. "You got bad vibes from him, too."

Zak snorted. "Vibes? Sure."

"What else do you call them?"

He didn't respond. He stopped walking like he'd hit a wall and stared at a group gathered around one of the tables on the porch.

She followed his gaze. "Oh."

His whole family was here. His parents, Grady and Paksima. His older sister, Jamila, and brother-in-law, Lance. His brother, Taj, and sister-in-law, Leslie. His youngest sister, Zara, and her fiancée, Chelsey.

And the girl he'd rescued in Afghanistan, his newly adopted sister, Tehani.

They noticed him and their conversations trailed off. He was frozen, unable to take that next step, but also unable to run away.

She entwined her fingers with his and tugged him forward. "Let's say hi."

"Zak! You came!" Tehani jumped up from her seat, her dark eyes glittering excitedly, her smile as bright as a sunbeam. Her English was almost perfect, with only the slightest accent. She'd learned fast in her two years as an American citizen. "I'm so glad you're here."

"Came for what?" he asked with a strange hollow note in his voice.

"It's Tehani's eighteenth birthday," Jamila said. "We all called you."

"Multiple times," Taj said with a roll of his eyes. "You could've answered and let us know you're not dead."

"Taj, shut up," Zara hissed. "You're not helping."

Paksima stood and reached for him. "Zakir." She said something in her native language and every muscle in his body tensed up like he was expecting an attack. He stared straight ahead as she hugged him, but Anna knew he wasn't seeing his family. He had that faraway look in his eyes again, like up on the mountain. He was back in Afghanistan, reliving horrors that nobody should ever have to endure.

When she didn't get a response, Paksima backed up a step and folded her hands in front of her mouth. Tears leaked from her eyes.

Grady wrapped an arm around his wife's shoulders and said in English, "How are you?"

Zak shook his head, and without another word, walked away. Paksima turned into her husband's arms and sobbed.

Tehani deflated into her seat while Jamila, Zara, and Chelsey tried to comfort her.

"I—" Helpless, Anna looked between his departing back and his family. "I'm sorry. This is my fault. I pushed him to come here, and he wasn't ready." She hadn't known about the birthday party, or else she wouldn't have suggested it. "I'll talk to him."

Taj shoved back his chair. "If he's just gonna keep coming around and hurting Mom, he can stay away. You hear that, you bastard?" he shouted across the parking lot and took a step like he was going to chase Zak down, but his wife and brother-in-law grabbed him, holding him back. "Stay the fuck away from us!"

"I'm sorry," Anna said again and ran after Zak.

He was waiting at the passenger door and jumped in the moment she unlocked her car. Ranger nuzzled his face, but even the dog's happiness at seeing him didn't penetrate his fog.

She slid in behind the wheel. "Zak..." She said nothing more for a handful of beats. "You should—"

"Please, don't." His voice was still empty and toneless. "I'll do whatever else you demand, but don't make *them* part of the conditions for keeping Ranger. Because I can't, okay? I can't. Not with them."

"I don't understand. Your family loves you. And that girl? You saved her. Not only that, but you brought her here and gave her opportunities she never would've had in her country. She adores you. You're her hero."

His jaw tightened. "Just take me home."

"Where you can drink yourself to death? Hell no." She studied him, waited for him to look at her. When he only continued staring straight ahead through the windshield, she sighed. "You don't like that word, do you? Hero?"

"It's thrown around too much. It's lost all meaning."

Shit. This was bad. This was the man she'd seen when he

answered the door earlier— hollow-eyed and on the brink of something disastrous. A man who thought he had nothing left to live for. She had to remind him that wasn't true. And Ranger, as good as he was for Zak, just wasn't enough. She had to find another way to connect with him.

There was one way she hadn't tried yet...

It was dangerous. She could—probably would—end up heartbroken again, but the still-simmering attraction between them was all she had left in her arsenal.

She had to try.

Because she knew without a doubt if she couldn't reach Zak soon, the next time he didn't show up for work, she'd find him dead.

Her stomach rolled at the thought.

She had to try.

chapter
twenty-one

ZAK ONLY REALIZED they weren't heading toward home when she pulled into the fast food drive-thru at the truck stop outside of town. He scowled at her. "What are you doing?"

"Getting food. I haven't eaten all day. What do you want?" she asked as she rolled down her window.

He didn't want anything. His stomach was in such tight knots he didn't think it'd even accept food right now. When he didn't respond, she shrugged and ordered cheeseburgers, fries, and drinks for them, and a plain burger for Ranger. She paid at the window, then passed him the bag and pointed the car in the opposite direction of either of their houses. He didn't bother asking where they were going. He was sure he'd hate whatever she had in mind and just silently watched the evening sun sink toward the ocean as they wound their way along Highway 1. She pulled into the lighthouse parking lot, which was packed with cars of tourists waiting for the sunset, and gathered a blanket from her trunk. She leashed Ranger, then stood beside the car, the blanket tossed over her shoulder and one hand on her hip.

"Well? You just going to sit here all night and let me starve?"

Grumbling under his breath, he got out of the car with the bag of food. Instead of dragging him down the path to the beach below the lighthouse like he thought, she chose one that wound up onto the cliffs overhead. It was a steep hike, and he was winded by the time they reached the picnic area at the top, but she still didn't stop. She let Ranger off his leash and slipped into the woods, following a barely there trail even higher. The dog bounded after her, having the time of his life on this impromptu hike.

Zak paused and leaned on a picnic table, sucking in several gasping lungfuls of air—fuck, he really had to start working out regularly again. When he finally caught up, he found her spreading the blanket out next to a steaming pool of water. A narrow waterfall burbled soothingly through the rocks over-head before cascading into the spring.

The ball of tension in his chest loosened. There was nobody else here but them.

"What are we doing here?"

She took the food bag from him and sat down. "Having a picnic in my favorite spot."

"I'm not talking about my family."

"I wasn't planning on talking. I'm eating."

He glanced back at the path they had taken. He could see glints of the setting sun on the ocean through the trees, but nothing more of the sunset. "It'll be dark soon."

"I have a flashlight. What, are you afraid of the dark?"

"I'm afraid of falling off a cliff in the dark like any rational person would be."

She unwrapped the burger for Ranger and baby-talked as she fed it to him. "Who's a good boy? Ranger's such a good boy."

Zak watched the dog devour the patty and winced. "That can't be good for him."

"Oh, relax. It's a treat. Good boys get treats." When he still didn't move from the path to join her, she arched a brow in obvious challenge. "*You* are not a good boy."

Heat curled through him. "You don't want me to be."

A smile flickered at the edge of her mouth, but she didn't confirm or deny as she dug in the fast food bag for her own burger. She took a bite and made an orgasmic sound that had all of his nerve endings bursting to painful life again, just like last time he'd kissed her.

His mouth went dry, and he grabbed one of the sodas, focusing on the trees, the spring, the waterfall, the dog—anywhere but on her—as he sucked it down. "Where are we?"

"Mm." She swallowed the bite she'd taken and wiped her mouth with a napkin. "My family's land."

He pulled up a mental map of town, and the geography wasn't adding up. The Rawlings ranch lands were north of Steam Valley and stretched eastward into the mountains from the coast. The lighthouse, and therefore this spring, were to the south of town.

"Don't hurt yourself." She grinned and popped a fry in her mouth. "Yep, the Rawlings own more than the ranch. It's the best kept secret in town." Her smile dimmed a wattage. "Thankfully."

He finally stepped off the path and lowered himself onto the blanket. "I take it the developers don't know?"

Her gaze snapped to his. "How do you know about them?"

"Small town, and the rumor mill has been working overtime, especially in the bars. Everyone's saying they want the ranch land for a resort, and everyone has an opinion about it."

She picked at the bun of her burger, ripping off a piece. "They want my house and Redwood Coast Rescue, but they're not getting either." She popped the bread in her mouth and looked at the waterfall. "And no, they don't know about this place. If they did, they'd want it, too. My several-times-over-great-grandfather bought all of this with a shell company he'd set up to launder money during the gold rush. The company's all legal now—Ash wouldn't have it any other way—but it would take Monarch years to dig through all the paperwork to find the owners. It's not worth it to them when they think they can bully poor little Anna Rawlings and her struggling dog rescue."

"They have no idea who they're up against," Zak said. "The stubbornest woman in the world."

She sighed. "Yeah, well. I may be stubborn, but I don't have unlimited funds like they do. Wish my however-many-greats-granddaddy had thought to put the ranch under the company's name, too, but..." She trailed off and shrugged. "It doesn't matter. They're not getting it, no matter what they threaten."

"They've been threatening you?"

She finished her burger and wadded up the wrapper. "You might as well know Monarch's taking me to court, saying I don't actually own the land. I volunteered the rescue for your community service because the judge who handled your case will also handle the property dispute. I thought if I could rehabilitate you, it would prove my rescue is more of an asset to the town than some fancy resort."

"Ah, so you're not as altruistic as I thought."

"Let's call it a mix of altruism and desperation."

"Unfortunately, you placed your bets on the wrong horse. I'm beyond help."

She met his gaze. "No, you're not."

"Anna Rawlings, the queen of lost causes," he muttered. Annnd this convo was getting damn uncomfortable, so he grabbed a handful of fries from the bag to avoid continuing it. They were cold but tasted good and he suddenly realized he *was* hungry. Starving. He'd been subsisting on a liquid diet and the occasional handful of stale cereal. He couldn't even remember the last time he ate actual food. Was it the sandwich she'd made for him?

Fuck. That was over a week ago.

He unwrapped his burger. Judging by her amusement, he must've made a noise similar to hers when he bit in, but he didn't care. At that moment, it was the best thing he'd ever tasted, and when it was gone, he wished he had another.

"Here." Anna took his burger wrapper and passed him the bag of cold fries. "Have my fries. I'm done."

She stuffed the wrappers and napkins in the small trash bag she'd brought from her car, then stood and stripped off her shirt.

He nearly choked on the fries. "What are you doing?"

"Getting in the hot spring. Why else would I hike all the way up here?" She pulled off her sports bra and let it drop onto her shirt. When she skimmed her pants down her legs, he averted his gaze.

She snorted a laugh. "Oh, c'mon, you've seen me naked lots of times."

"Fifteen years ago."

"Nothing's changed other than my weight."

Yeah, right. From the glimpse he'd gotten before he looked away, a lot had changed. She was no longer the skinny teenager he remembered, and that extra weight she mentioned had filled her out in all the right places. Her breasts would overflow his hands now and her ass...

He shifted, suddenly uncomfortably hot.

Fuck, he wasn't hungry anymore. At least not for cold French fries.

She was toying with him, playing on the still simmering sexual attraction between them. "I know what you're doing."

"Swimming?"

"You're trying to distract me."

"Is it working?"

He heard a splash and risked a glance in her direction. She stood under the waterfall, her head tilted up toward the spray. She was beautiful. Ethereal, like a creature of myth.

His breath caught in his chest. "Yeah, it's working."

chapter
twenty-two

ANNA WALKED BACK across the pool toward him, her soft laughter like a siren's call, beckoning him to his doom.

He squeezed his eyes shut and mentally grabbed onto his quickly unraveling thread of control with both hands. "Anna, stop. You don't want to go there again with me. I broke your heart last time—on purpose—because it was easier to walk away."

"I know. So now it's my turn to get revenge and break yours."

His eyes popped open at that. "I'm already broken. There's nothing left."

"We'll see."

God, she didn't look real standing there in the pool of clear water with steam swirling around her. Her hair curled over her shoulders and water dripped from the ends, trailing down her body. He wanted to lick it away.

Using the tip of her finger, she traced one droplet's trail between her full breasts. "What are you staring at?"

She was shameless. Completely comfortable in her own skin, and he couldn't decide if he hated her for it or wanted her even more. "A woman who doesn't know when to stop."

"Do you want me to stop?" Her hand stopped moving just below her navel, fingers teasing the red curls at the vee of her legs. "Or would you rather I come closer so you can touch me? Warm me up? That waterfall was cold."

Even from where he sat, he could see the goosebumps on her skin. Her nipples puckered to tight little peaks as she continued closing the distance between them. An erection—his first in... Jesus, he didn't even remember how long—swelled painfully against his fly. He wanted to cover her body with his and warm away those goosebumps using the kind of hot friction that ended with both of them coming.

She stopped in front of him and smiled seductively as she picked up his hand and splayed it on her hip. He shuddered at the contact and surged up just as she bent down, their lips crashing together in a desperate click of teeth and dance of tongues. She straddled his lap, digging her hands into his too-long hair, her nails biting into his scalp. It felt like she was punishing him for something—missing his community service, scaring her, walking away from his family. He didn't care to know her reasons. Whatever they were, he was one hundred percent on board. He was an asshole of the highest caliber and deserved all the punishment she could dream up. Especially if it lit him on fire like this.

He wasn't numb anymore. When she touched him, he could *feel* again. The scratch of her nails, the bite of her teeth on his lower lip, her cold, wet body grinding against his throbbing cock. He felt all of it, and it didn't make him want to eat a bullet or drive off a cliff. He wanted more.

He reached between her legs and found her soaked—and not from the spring. She circled her hips against his hand as his fingers dipped inside and the pull of her walls sucking at him almost made him rocket off right then and there in his pants. It had been a long time since he'd last had sex. Too long. He would not have any staying power, so he had to make sure she came first.

Groaning, he broke the kiss and captured her breast in his mouth, giving her nipple a hard tug with his teeth. She gasped and arched, pushing his fingers deeper into her body. He pressed his thumb against her clit and watched her ride herself to climax, loving the way she moved against him and the sounds she made as she came.

She was a good girl in the streets, but a bad girl in bed. He'd forgotten that about her. The summer they'd spent together, she'd been wild and up for anything. They'd done things together that, to this day, he hadn't done with any other woman.

"Fuck," he whispered against her skin. "I want you, Anna. I've always fucking wanted you. Never stopped."

She stared down at him with sleepy eyes and a satisfied smirk. "Bet you can't make me do that again with just your cock."

Challenge accepted.

He unzipped so fast he was lucky he didn't pinch himself — but stopped her before she could slide down his length. "We don't have a condom."

She rubbed teasingly against his tip. "I can't get pregnant."

That was all he needed to hear. He grabbed her hips and pulled her down on him as he thrust up. He lost himself in the rhythm of their joining until every nerve ending in his body exploded in a brilliant flash of heat and color. He had no idea if he made her orgasm again, but he came so hard he thought his body might rip in half. He went blind and deaf and lost all sense of self, of sanity, as his world narrowed to her. She was the oxygen that filled his lungs. The water in his blood. She was everything he needed to survive.

He wrapped his arms around her and hugged her tight, resting his head against her breasts, listening to the gallop of her heartbeat. If he let her go, he'd float off into the black, endless numbness again.

He couldn't to go back there.

Without a doubt, he'd die there if he went back.

He was shaking.

It was the first thing Anna realized when she came back to herself from another mind-shattering orgasm. He'd been wild and desperate, pounding into her like his life depended on it. All she'd been able to do was hang on and hope he didn't buck her off. Then he hit a spot inside her that sent her flying. She hadn't known she could come from penetration. She'd always needed clitoral stimulation in the past, and her dare had been nothing but a sneaky way to get him to drop his guard—and his pants.

But that orgasm? She'd experienced nothing like it before. Her body still hummed and buzzed, and mini firecrackers exploded across her skin. She wasn't cold anymore, that was for sure.

But Zak was. Even though he was still fully clothed, he shook like he was trapped in the middle of an ice storm without winter gear.

"Zak?" she whispered, combing a hand through his hair. "What's wrong?"

His arms tightened around her, and he muttered something that sounded like, "I can't go back."

Her throat closed up, and she cradled his head against her chest. "We don't have to right now. We still have time before it gets dark. We can stay right here if you want."

"No, I—" He sucked in a breath and let it out in a rush

that sounded dangerously close to a sob. "I can't go back to the darkness. The emptiness. The numbness. I was drowning in it until you. I *feel* with you. And I'm so fucking afraid if I let you go, I'll sink into that cold nothing again and won't come back up. I almost killed myself last night. If Ranger hadn't shown up when he did—" He broke off.

She'd known it, had seen it all over him when he answered the door this afternoon, but hearing him confirm it ripped through her like a serrated blade. She looked at Ranger. He lay several feet away, watching them with an expression of doggie annoyance.

Thank you, she told him silently. He lifted his head, and she saw understanding in his yellow eyes. "I've never been so glad he's an escape artist."

Zak tightened his grip on her and sniffed like he was trying to hold back a flood of emotion. "You're right. I am a coward. It's easier to walk away from my family than talk to them. It's easier to drink myself stupid than face you or my therapy group. It's easier to kill myself than deal with what happened to me."

Oh, God, she regretted calling him that. "That's not true. You're the bravest man I know."

"Brave men don't take the easy way out. I've never taken the easy way in my life, so why is it all I can think about now? I'm in a fucking tailspin and I'm not strong enough to pull myself out. I've tried."

"Zak." She lifted his chin with her hand, unsurprised to see his lashes spiked with moisture and tear tracks on his face. She kissed them away. "You don't have to face this alone. You have me. You've *always* had me. That's why I brought you up here. To remind you of us, the way we used to be. We could be that again. I'd like for there to be an us again. You have *so much* to live for."

Ranger gave an exasperated huff, and she smiled over at

him. "And you have a strong support network now. You have Ranger, Dr. Firestone and the rest of your therapy group, your family. You even have Ash. He may not admit it, but he worries about you nonstop. We all do. We're all here for you, so if the darkness swallows you again, all you have to do is reach out. Just reach out."

He trailed his fingers down her arm but stopped inches from touching her hand. "I'm reaching," he said, voice raw. "I need help."

Heart in her throat, she closed the distance between their hands and laced her fingers with his. "And I'm right here. I'm not letting you drown."

part two
found

We have all known the long loneliness, and we have found that
the answer is community.

Dorothy Day

HAVE YOU SEEN US?

BELLADONNA "BELLA" EVELYN LOWE

POPPY LINEA LOWE

AGE: 16
HEIGHT: 5 FT 4 IN
WEIGHT: 115 LBS
HAIR: BLOND DREADLOCKS WITH DARK ROOTS
RACE: MIXED
EYES: BROWN
CLOTHES: GRAY HOODED SWEATSHIRT, RED FLANNEL, BLACK LEGGINGS, AND COMBAT BOOTS

AGE: 5
HEIGHT: 3 FT 6 IN
WEIGHT: 30 LBS
HAIR: BLOND, STRAIGHT
RACE: WHITE
EYES: BLUE
CLOTHES: PINK PUFFER JACKET, PURPLE LEGGINGS, AND FLOWER RAIN BOOTS

BOTH GIRLS WERE LAST SEEN ON OCTOBER 16TH OF THIS YEAR AT LOST ROCKS STATE PARK CAMPSITE A. THEY WERE ABDUCTED BY THEIR MOTHER, JESSICA LOWE, FROM THEIR HOME IN TUCSON, ARIZONA.

IF YOU HAVE ANY INFORMATION THAT CAN HELP FIND THEM, PLEASE CONTACT THEIR FATHER, JAKE BECKETT, AT (123) 456-7890.

chapter
twenty-three

ZAK SPENT every night of the next two weeks at Anna's and almost never went home, except to grab more clothes. In truth, he was afraid to. The last night he'd spent there had nearly been his last on earth. If he went back, would he slide into that darkness again?

He wasn't certain enough about his newfound will to live to test it.

Besides, he enjoyed every second in Anna's bed, where they fucked like horny teenagers until they fell into an exhausted, sated sleep, usually with his cock still nestled between her legs. He liked waking up beside her, having breakfast with her, and then walking across the driveway to the barn to help her care for the dogs. He was slowly earning the trust of the poor burned golden retriever, Matilda. He had fun playing with Raszta, the mop dog. He loved training Ranger in cadaver detection and worked with him daily.

For the first time since he made the decision to blow his cover and rescue Tehani, he felt alive.

The only kink in all the happy was Ash. He was pissed about the rekindled relationship and uncharacteristically vocal about his feelings. It didn't seem to bother Anna, so he tried to let it roll off him, too.

He'd never admit it, but Ash's intense hatred of him hurt.

Yeah, he'd been a dick since he got home and had made Ash's job a hundred times harder, but a few bar fights couldn't possibly be all that was behind the guy's simmering rage. Something more fueled it, but any time he brought it up to Anna, she shrugged it off as Ash being Ash.

"He'll come around," she said. "He's just being a protective ass. Give him time."

Greer Wilde called every day to check on him. At first, it annoyed Zak, but then he started to look forward to their evening conversations. Reconnecting felt good, and he was touched beyond words when he was the first person Greer called with the news that he and his wife were expecting. The man had been his commander, his brother-in-arms, and their bond was formed in the blood and dirty deeds of an endless war that had left them both shattered in different ways. If Greer was okay enough now to have a happy marriage and become a father, then maybe there was hope for Zak.

Maybe he wasn't a lost cause.

Talking to Greer was also better therapy than the court-mandated group shit. He was one of the few people who knew exactly what Zak had faced overseas, and he also knew when *not* to bring it up—unlike the damn therapy group.

Zak dreaded every session.

As Sawyer predicted, Donovan returned and said nothing about his blow-up. He simply arrived early for the next session with a drywall repair kit to fix the hole, then sat down like nothing happened. The sessions carried on like usual after that, with one of them doing the majority of the talking each time. The day it was Pierce's turn, Zak was lost. He really had to learn some sign language.

But, this morning, everyone seemed off—quieter, more

withdrawn. Even Dr. Firestone wasn't her usual cheerful self as she set her bag down and let Alfie out to use his psychic powers. He sniffed around the circle, then stopped, as he so often did, in front of Veronica's chair. She scooped him up with a muffled sob.

The good mood Zak had been riding all morning suffocated in the thick cloud of depression. Dammit, he didn't need them dragging him down when his good moods were so few and far between. "What the hell is up with you all?"

Dr. Firestone cleared her throat. "There was another member of our group who stopped coming right before you joined us—"

"Christina Jimenez," Veronica said and hugged Alfie, burying her face between his ears. "She was found dead this morning with a needle in her arm. She sat where you sit now."

The news hit Zak like a blow, knocking all the air out of his lungs.

Someone else had once sat in his seat.

Someone who just lost her battle with her demons.

Donovan pressed his fingers to his eyes. "I thought Chrissy was off that shit."

Pierce signed something. Nobody bothered translating, so Zak had no idea what he said.

"Yeah, I don't get it, either," Sawyer said, presumably answering Pierce. "She was doing so good. She was healing, and then she just stops showing up out of the blue? It doesn't make sense."

"You don't heal from the shit she went through," Veronica whispered.

"She never told us what she went through."

"She was raped by a commanding officer and when she tried to get help, command kicked her out and silenced her." She shook her head and tears spilled from her dark eyes. "You don't heal from that."

Donovan dropped his hand from his eyes and stared at Veronica for a long moment. "Fuck," he said with an edge of anger in his voice. "You're talking from experience. That's what happened to you, too, isn't it?"

Veronica looked at Dr. Firestone, who nodded encouragement. "It's time, Vee."

"Okay." She drew a deep, ragged breath. "Three of my fellow airmen held me down at gunpoint and—" The words seemed to catch in her throat, and she coughed. "They—they gang-raped me. Men who I thought were friends, who were supposed to have my six, and they violated me. And like Chrissy, when I tried to report it, they claimed I wanted it. I was branded a slut and a troublemaker and pushed out of the Air Force."

Pierce popped to his feet and paced, signing furiously. Zak didn't have to know the language to know the guy was cursing a blue streak. There were a lot of middle fingers being thrown around and gestures he recognized.

Donovan had gone deadly silent.

Sawyer shook his head. "You didn't trust us enough to tell us."

"Can you blame me? I can't trust any man anymore. Not even my dad or my best friend since childhood. This group—" She broke off and looked at Dr. Firestone again.

"Go ahead," the doctor urged. "Tell them."

"This group is exposure therapy for me."

"We'd *never* hurt you." Donovan's jaw was clenched so tightly, it was amazing he got any words out. "We don't hurt women here."

She lifted a shoulder. "I thought the same thing about the men who attacked me. Look, you're not my friends. We'll never be friends. I'm only here because I need help, and Dr. Firestone suggested it would be good for me."

I need help.

Zak looked away, the words echoing uncomfortably in his head. He'd said the same to Anna at the hot spring two weeks ago. "We don't have to be friends to help you."

Everyone looked at him. Or, in Sawyer's case, toward his voice.

"What was that?" Dr. Firestone asked.

Shit. He should've kept his mouth shut. He rubbed his suddenly sweaty palms on his thighs. "She doesn't have to see us as friends for us to be here for her. We just have to wait until she's ready to reach out." He met Veronica's gaze across the room. "I'll be here when you're ready."

"Me, too," Sawyer said.

Pierce nodded.

"Yeah, friends or not, you're one of us," Donovan said. "We'll always have your six."

Several beats passed in silence.

Dr. Firestone blinked. "Well, thank you, Zak. That was very insightful."

He cracked a small smile. He'd smiled a lot more over the last couple of weeks, but it still felt weird on his face. "I've learned a few things."

Veronica set Alfie down and grabbed her jacket from the back of her chair. She ignored them all, except for the doctor. "Can I leave?"

"It's not a prison. You're free to come and go as you please." Dr. Firestone also stood. "In fact, in honor of Chrissy, we'll call it a little early today and I want you all to go out into the community and do something in her memory—clean up the beach, volunteer at the soup kitchen. Let's spread some joy in her name."

Donovan lingered behind after everyone else left. He leaned against the wall by the door and watched Zak fold and stack the chairs with suspicion. "Okay, what happy pills are you taking and where can I get some?"

"I'm not on drugs."

"You're not drinking either."

"How the fuck do you know?"

"You don't smell like a distillery anymore."

Zak scowled at him and moved on to dealing with the coffeepot. He tapped the used filter into the garbage and took the nearly full pot to the sink to dump it.

Donovan pushed away from the wall and trailed him to the employee break room. "And then that shit you said to Veronica? It was exactly the right thing, exactly what she needed to hear, but none of us who have known her for months thought to say it. So, yeah, it's got me wondering what changed? What's the magic pill? Because I've been coming here for almost a year and every fucking day is still a struggle."

"Nothing's changed."

Donovan's eyes narrowed. "Bullshit. You're different."

The side door leading out to the agility yard opened and Anna walked in with Matilda on a leash. Sasha followed and the two women carried on a conversation about the dog's progress as they led her back to C-Wing. Anna waved to him before they disappeared down the hall.

Zak smiled. He couldn't help it. It was an involuntary response every time he saw her.

"Ah." Donovan slapped him on the back. "I get it. Not a magic pill. Magic pussy. I should get me some of that."

Jealousy sizzled through him like a lightning strike. He shrugged off Donovan's hand and whirled on the guy, fully intending to punch him if he said another word. "Make a move on her and you won't have to worry about your scrambled brain anymore. It'll be on the wall."

A grin spread across Donovan's hard face. "Nah, no worries there. Redheads aren't my thing. The curvy one she was with, though? Damn, I could make some magic with her."

The asshole had been poking at him on purpose, trying to

get a rise out of him. And it had worked. He couldn't shake the lingering jealousy. It buzzed under his skin, making him twitchy.

Emotions.

Jesus.

After being numb for so long, he wasn't used to their intensity and never knew how to handle them when they took him in a chokehold like that.

He grumbled and turned his attention back to cleaning the coffeepot, scrubbing it out harder than necessary. "Don't you have to go spread joy somewhere else that's not here?"

Grin still in place, Donovan opened his arms wide and backed toward the door. "Man, I spread joy everywhere I go."

"Yeah, when you leave."

Donovan snorted a laugh and gave him the finger before shoving through the door.

chapter
twenty-four

ZAK SAT at the kitchen table, scrolling through a news article about Christina Jimenez's death, when Anna came back to the house for lunch.

"Oh, you made mac and cheese! Thank God. I'm starving." She leaned over his shoulder and stole a bite from his bowl. "What are you reading?"

He closed the laptop. "It's nothing. How's Matilda?"

She crossed to the stove to scoop some pasta for herself. "Sasha doesn't think she'll get full range of motion back in her front leg because of all the scar tissue, but, honestly, it hasn't slowed her down much. The daily agility runs have helped, and she *loves* them. That dog's happiest when she's zooming. I'm even seeing some of her personality peeking out. She's sassy and has a high prey drive. She might be an excellent candidate for search and rescue if we can work through her trust issues."

"I'll go play with her again this afternoon after Ranger's training session. I think she's starting to like me."

"She more than likes you. She's getting a bit of a doggie crush on you."

"Who can blame her? I mean, look at me." He gestured to

himself. "A one-legged soldier with a drinking problem and PTSD out the wazoo. I'm a catch."

"I think so."

He grabbed the coffee he'd forgotten about and took a drink. It was cold. He made a face and pushed it aside. "And I still think you need your head examined for taking me back."

"What can I say? I'm a sucker for lost causes." Anna leaned against the counter with her bowl in hand and took a bite of the pasta as she eyed the laptop. "So, how was therapy?"

He raised a shoulder. "You know. Therapy."

"Uh-huh." She came over to the table, set her bowl down, and before he realized her intention, she snatched the computer.

"Oh," she breathed when she saw the article and sank into the chair beside him. "Chrissy. I'm guessing they heard the news then?"

"Yeah. Everyone was pretty torn up about it."

She shook her head, closed the laptop, and dragged her bowl over in front of her. "It's so sad. I didn't know her well, but she seemed like a good person. She volunteered here occasionally, and the dogs loved her."

She sat where you sit now.

Zak poked at his macaroni, but his appetite was gone. "Do you think she did it on purpose?"

"What, overdose?" She paused with her spoon halfway to her mouth, considering it. "I didn't know her well enough to say, but she *was* an addict and there's been a rash of fentanyl-related deaths lately. It could be she just wanted to get high and bought from the wrong person. Why do you ask?"

"Everyone was so shocked. They said she seemed like she was doing well, healing, and then she suddenly stopped showing up to group and..." He motioned to the laptop. "Three weeks later, she's dead."

She set down her spoon. "You're afraid you'll backslide, too."

"It's not an irrational fear."

"No, it's not. But you have something she didn't..." She reached for his hand and laced their fingers together. "Me."

"How did I get so fucking lucky?" He leaned over the table to kiss her but was interrupted by an annoyed throat clearing.

"Ash," he muttered and sank back into his seat. "Great timing, as usual."

A muscle ticked in Ash's jaw as he glowered at them from the kitchen doorway.

Anna smiled brightly at her brother. "Did you need something?"

He growled and started to turn away. "No."

"Oh, c'mon, Ash. Don't be like that. You came here to vent. I can see it all over you. So, sit down and vent."

Ash dragged a hand through his disheveled hair. He was usually all buttoned-up and militarily neat about his appearance, but the guy looked haggard. His beard was overdue for a trim and dark shadows lined his eyes. He hesitated a beat, then grudgingly sank into a chair and slapped a wrinkled flyer down on the table between them.

It was the missing poster for Bella and Poppy Lowe.

Shit. Zak had completely forgotten about the one the girls' father had given him outside of The Grove. He picked it up and studied the two photos. Once again, his gaze was drawn to the older girl, Bella. Why was she so familiar?

"Jake Beckett's been on my ass about his daughters," Ash said. "He refuses to accept the case has gone cold, and I don't blame him for wanting answers, but... there aren't any. I have no leads and absolutely zero evidence the girls or their mother are still in the area. I can't even say for sure if they're alive or dead. We had the blood at the campsite tested and it matched

Jessica Lowe's blood type, but DNA confirmation's gonna take weeks. I've done everything I can officially. It's not even my case anymore—it's FBI jurisdiction because the kids were taken over state lines, but they are doing jack-shit with it and now Beckett's been investigating it himself. He's going around accusing people and causing problems in the community, but I can't take my deputies away from active investigations for his wild goose chases."

"We can do another search," Anna suggested.

Ash shook his head. "I can't put any more department resources toward this, especially now, with the Jimenez case."

Zak looked up from the poster. "Chrissy Jimenez's death wasn't just an overdose?"

"It probably was, but as an unattended death, it has to be investigated."

He was lying. Or at least avoiding the entire truth. Zak recognized his tells from when they were kids. His left eyelid always twitched slightly when he lied. "What aren't you telling us? Is there a connection between the Lowe family and Jimenez?"

He raised his hands in a halt gesture. "I can't comment. The media are already swarming because of the circumstances of Jimenez's dismissal from the Army, and I can't risk leaks. It's going to turn into a circus."

"Maybe it needs to be a circus," Zak said. "What happened to her wasn't right. The Army should be held accountable."

Ash scowled, and it was very obvious he didn't want to admit he agreed just because it was Zak who had said it. But, after a stubborn second, he nodded. "Yes, but that leaves me playing politics, and those girls are still out there somewhere with nobody but their dad looking for them. And there's something off about that man. I get the sense he's lying to me every time I talk to him."

Anna gnawed on her lower lip and looked at Zak, then at

the flyer he still held. "What if I set up a training exercise at the campground? We can see how Zak and Ranger and some of the other new teams do in a real-world setting, and maybe we'll get lucky."

"That's overly optimistic, AJ."

"It's better than doing nothing."

He was silent a moment. "Yeah," he finally said with a sigh and pushed out of his chair. "You're right. I need to get back to work, but let's do it. Set up the training exercise and let me know when it is. I want to be there."

That night, Zak dreamed for the first time in weeks, but it was different from his usual nightmares. He wasn't mired in it, reliving pain or torture, but instead watched the scenes play out in bits and pieces like a stuttering old movie reel.

A foggy road.

A camper van.

A ghostly, wide-eyed face in the harsh splash of headlights.

"I'm so sorry. I'm so, so sorry. I didn't see you! I called for help. Hang on."

A girl with a jeweled nose and dreadlocks.

A bloody hand gripping hers tightly.

"Please. I can't stay. They're coming to help you, but I can't be here. I don't have a license. They'll take Poppy from me..."

Zak bolted upright, his breath caught in his throat.

The girl.

He scrambled out of bed.

"Zak?" Anna sat up and turned on the light. She blinked at him, pushing her hair back from her face. "What's wrong?"

He hopped over to their pile of clothes on the floor and

dug through until he found his jeans. He'd folded the missing persons flyer earlier and stuffed it into his back pocket. Now he pulled it out, flattened it on the dresser, and studied the older girl's face. She didn't have a nose ring in the picture, but he knew she'd gotten one since it was taken.

It *was* her.

Bella.

The girl who had witnessed his first suicide attempt.

The girl who had saved him by calling for help and holding his hand until the last second before that help arrived. She'd kept him anchored, kept him from giving up.

"Jesus," he whispered and leaned on the dresser as his knee threatened to give out.

Anna came up behind him and flattened her hand over the ropes of scar tissue on his back. When they first started sleeping together, he hadn't liked her seeing or touching his scars, but now he found the weight of her hand a comfort.

"Did you have a nightmare?" she asked softly.

"No. At least, not about Afghanistan." He tapped the flyer. "This was the girl who called for help the night of my accident."

Her eyes widened. "The lipstick."

He glanced over, eyebrow raised. "Lipstick?"

"I always wondered..." She shook her head. "I found you that night because there was a trail of random objects with lipstick arrows on them pointing down from the road to you. We never figured out who did that."

"She saved me." Zak stared at Bella's photo and certainty bloomed in his chest. "She's alive."

"Oh, Zak. You can't know that."

"No, she's alive. She lived with an abusive, drug-addicted mother, who flew into rages at the drop of a hat, and she took all the beatings without complaint to protect her younger sister. That family at the campground next to theirs told us as much the night of the first search. Bella also got a job off the books to support herself and provide for the kid. And she pointed you to me, using whatever she had on hand to create a trail." He tapped the photo again with his knuckle. "This girl's tenacious and smart. She's a survivor. She's alive and wherever she is, she's still protecting her sister." He lifted his gaze to Anna's. "We have to find them."

chapter
twenty-five

IT HAD BEEN over two weeks since Mom died. Actually, almost three now. Nineteen days.

Bella kept track of the passing time by scratching marks into the wood paneling of their prison with a nail she'd wiggled loose from the floorboards.

And she still didn't know who Hoodie Man was or what he wanted.

As promised, he didn't hurt them. After depositing them in this basement room, he never laid a hand on them again. He locked them in and only returned to give them food three times a day or bring them fresh clothes and bed linens. He never really spoke—he acted like he wanted to, but couldn't figure out what to say—and always seemed sad.

As far as prisons went, this was a comfortable one. The room was large, with a plush sectional sofa, two soft beds, a full bathroom, and a huge entertainment system. Poppy was dazzled by the TV, the wide selection of streaming services, and the overflowing bookshelves. There were DVDs, board games, puzzles and all kinds of books—but not the one about the fae prince that Mom had destroyed, dammit.

If she died without finding out the ending, she was going to be pissed.

There was a galley kitchen along one wall with and a line of cupboards filled with snacks and a small fridge stocked with water, juice, and soda. Their first day here, Bella had checked to see if there were any knives in the drawers, but Hoodie Man had removed anything she could use as a weapon.

Compared to the way they had been living, this place was like a luxury resort. Poppy had never seen anything like it in her young life, and Bella managed to convince her they were on vacation. Luckily, she didn't seem to remember anything from the night Mom died.

Every morning when Hoodie Man brought their breakfast —with plastic cutlery, of course—he asked if there was anything else they needed or wanted. It was weird. He seemed to care about their comfort and was probably the nicest kidnapper in the crime's history.

But she knew from Mom's mood swings that could change in an instant. Nobody good kept two girls locked in a basement. It was only a matter of time until they saw his true nature, so she spent every free moment plotting an escape.

For all the good it'd done her.

Nineteen days and she still hadn't come up with a solid plan.

She knew they were still in Steam Valley. He'd apologetically blindfolded her after leaving the campgrounds, but she had a vague idea of the distance they'd traveled and knew they'd gone up in elevation. They were up on Murder Mountain. Maybe they were even close enough to Rainbow Rodriguez's pot farm to make a run for it.

Problem was, Hoodie Man always kept the door locked. It was a heavy door, too. Not something she could easily kick through, like in the movies—she'd tried and hurt her ankle.

The room had windows, but they were the thick glass

block kind that allowed light in and didn't open. She couldn't see out and nobody could see in. She'd tried breaking through them at the end of the first week and only busted up her knuckles.

Hoodie Man had not been amused either of the times he'd had to patch her up, but he'd been gentle about it. As he'd bandaged her split knuckles, she'd glanced toward the First Aid kit and thought about lunging for it. There were scissors in there—she'd seen them when he cut open the package of sterile gauze. But he was a big man, with hands more than double the size of hers, and they were comically tiny scissors. The only way they'd do any real damage was if she got him in the eye or something.

Wasn't worth the risk.

And, besides, she didn't really want to hurt him.

He didn't look like a killer. He was handsome, with sharp cheekbones and skin on the lighter side of black. His dark eyes were kind and his touch always gentle.

"Why are you doing this?" She glanced toward Poppy, who was enthralled with the TV and not paying attention. Still, she lowered her voice. "Why did you kill Mom?"

He winced. "I loved your mother."

"But you murdered her."

He said nothing in reply and scooped the bandage wrappers into the trash.

"Who are you?"

He exhaled hard and closed the First Aid kit. "It's... complicated."

She stared after him when he left, a weird empty ache blooming in her chest. She rubbed at it and scoffed at herself.

God. Can you say Stockholm syndrome?

Okay, next plan: somehow get a hold of his phone.

She had bounced around California long enough to know basements were rare in the state, so she could easily direct police to this place if she could call 9-1-1. A house on Murder Mountain with a basement that had glass brick windows. There couldn't be that many.

But how to get his phone?

And was there even a signal here?

She was on the couch, mulling over the problem while Poppy watched *Lilo and Stitch* for the hundredth time, when the door opened and someone other than Hoodie Man peeked inside.

Her blood ran cold.

Jake.

He'd found them.

Was he who Hoodie Man had been waiting for all this time?

He stepped into the room, and the door didn't shut all the way behind him. "Hi, Bella." Then he looked at Poppy with a smile and everything in her screamed, *no!* Mom had been a shitty mother, but the one thing she'd done right was get Poppy as far away from this man as possible.

She didn't think, just acted on pure, savage instinct. She exploded out of her seat and plowed into him. He hadn't been expecting it, and fell backwards with a forced exhale. His head hit the edge of the open door and his eyes rolled back. He went limp.

Bella grabbed her sister's hand. "Let's go!"

Poppy pulled away and looked back and forth from Jake to the TV. "My movie's not over."

She couldn't take the time to explain. She scooped the girl up and jumped over Jake's motionless body. Her foot slid in the pool of blood spreading under his head.

Was he still breathing?

Had she killed him?

Oh, God. Oh, God. Oh, God.

She ran upstairs, pausing for a heartbeat at the top to listen for movement. Nothing. Hoodie Man wasn't here. He was too big to move silently in the old house with all the creaky floors.

This was her chance.

She sucked in a breath, hugged Poppy tighter, and ran.

chapter
twenty-six

THE TRAINING EXERCISE went off without a hitch. All teams performed well, but Zak and Ranger were exceptional. If they kept this up, they'd be ready for certification in record time.

But nobody found any scent that she hadn't planted.

Anna didn't know why she was disappointed. It had been a long shot, but she'd hoped having more teams scouring the area would produce something actionable. She hated seeing Ash so twisted up over this case. He was looking more haggard with each passing day.

As the exercise wrapped up, she joined him next to his Tahoe in the parking lot. He was dressed casually today in jeans and a sweatshirt because he technically wasn't on duty, but her brother didn't know how to take a day off.

"I'm sorry."

"Don't be." He shrugged. "We both knew there was nothing here to find. If there had been, Winston would've led us to it that first night." He smiled down at her dog and gave his head a pat. "Nobody has a better nose than this handsome boy." He straightened and nodded across the parking lot, where Zak was playing with Ranger, rewarding him for a job well done. "Except for maybe that dog. He's something else."

"They make a great team, don't they?"

Ash slid her a sideways glance. "I hope you know what you're doing with him."

"Of course I do. Dogs are my life. Ranger's—"

"Don't play dumb. You know what I'm talking about. You and Zak." The constant frown he'd been wearing lately deepened and creases formed on his forehead. "It's dangerous."

Her heart went all gooey as Zak's laughter carried across the lot. She looked at them again and saw man and dog racing toward the beach as fast as his prosthesis allowed. "It's what he needs."

"What about what *you* need?"

She didn't reply because she didn't dare tell him the truth: she loved Zak. She adored his sarcasm and the smirk he wore when he was trying not to smile. His laugh, as rusty as it was, never failed to make her heart sing.

She loved that he was comfortable enough with her to show the vulnerability he hid from everyone else behind biting words and scowls. She wanted to hold him through all of his rough nights and soothe all of his nightmares.

And, of course, his single-minded focus on her pleasure in bed was off-the-charts amazing.

She loved his stubbornness, his grit, his heart. God, he had so much heart. She saw it every day when he interacted with the dogs.

In truth, she had always loved him. Never stopped. And, right now, her needs didn't matter until he was healthy again.

Which Ash definitely didn't want to hear.

Luckily, the radio in his Tahoe chirped with the dispatcher's voice, saving her from having to come up with an answer her brother would be satisfied with.

Ash leaned through the open passenger window to grab the mike. "Rawlings, here. Go ahead."

She wandered away to let him handle the call. "Let's go down to the beach, too, huh?" she said to Winston.

He wagged and bounded ahead. "Beach" was one of his favorite words and he ran laps around her, zooming to the beach and back as she strolled down the path winding through bleached piles of driftwood.

Zak and Ranger were all the way at the far end of the beach, down by the jetty where Razorrock River spilled into the ocean. She started toward them, figuring she'd meet them when they turned back.

Except they didn't turn back.

Ranger skidded to a halt and his nose shot into the air. He veered off the beach into the thick woods along the river, beyond the border of the state park's land.

Zak didn't hesitate to follow.

Did they have a scent?

Anna broke into a run. Winston gave a joyous bark and shot out ahead of her.

Maybe it was nothing.

It was probably nothing, but nobody had searched that area along the river because it was remote, mountainous, heavily forested terrain outside the state park's border. While it was only about a two-mile walk away on the beach, it was at least five times that distance by car on steep, twisty logging roads. Too dangerous to send teams out there without concrete evidence saying that was where they needed to search, and nothing pointed them in that direction. All the information they had indicated a vehicle was involved in the family's disappearance, so she'd focused search efforts on the easily accessible roads around the campgrounds. Hell, none of the dogs there could've even caught a scent from the river due to the geography of the area. Sharp cliffs rimmed the park to the north and east, creating a textbook dead zone at the campground for any scent originating from outside the park's border.

That was why Winston had circled aimlessly during that first search. He couldn't find anything other than the blood on the ground in front of him because all other scents were riding the wind on the cliffs over their heads.

As Winston neared the spot where Zak and Ranger had disappeared off the beach, he also skidded to a halt and lifted his head, his nose working overtime. He looked back at her, his expressive eyebrows raised in question, his tail starting a slow wag. He had a scent and knew this game. He was just checking in with her to make sure it was the game she wanted him to play.

"Yes, Winston. Good boy! Go. Find the napoo."

He put his nose to the ground, sniffed back and forth along the tree line, then plunged into the forest in the exact spot Zak and Ranger had.

The terrain was unforgivingly steep and slippery. She was struggling to keep up with her dog and couldn't imagine how Zak had managed it.

After nearly forty minutes of searching with no sign of Zak or Ranger, she wondered if they had gotten lost. Dammit, would she have to pull in teams to search for them, too? They were still training. Zak might not recognize when Ranger was off track or know how to redirect him. Ranger could just be chasing an animal.

Except Winston was on the scent, too, and he knew better.

They'd moved inland, and the beach was well behind them now. She followed her dog up another steep hill and found herself on an abandoned logging road. Up ahead, Ranger trotted around with his blue rope toy as Zak knelt, staring at something off the side of the road.

Winston surged toward them, circled Zak and Ranger,

then came charging back to her, full of doggie excitement. He made the loop again and again until she caught up. He was telling her found the napoo.

This close, even her inferior human nose could smell death.

She tossed him his favorite ball in reward, then crouched next to Zak. There, in the ferns a few yards from the road, was a mound of freshly dug earth covered with a fringed shawl in a bright southwestern print. A bloated, blackened human arm in an advanced state of decay poked out of the shallow grave.

"That shawl..." Zak glanced over at her, then back at the body. "Ranger found her. Jessica Lowe."

He sounded amazed by that fact.

"You *both* found her." She stood and surveyed the road with her hands on her hips. This section was little more than faint ruts in the mud, and who knew what the rest of the road looked like? It was going to be hell getting a crime scene crew here, but that was for her brother to figure out. "Leash the dogs so they don't disturb anything. We need Ash and more search teams up here to look for the girls."

"The girls are alive," Zak said with absolute certainty.

She ached to believe him. "God, I hope so."

chapter
twenty-seven

ZAK WAS EXHAUSTED.

It was the bone-deep, every-muscle-aching kind of exhaustion that came with long hours of physical labor and took him back to his days as a young soldier in Ranger School.

But he was also exhilarated.

His dog had found Jessica Lowe.

Yeah, yeah, Ash had cautioned not to jump to conclusions. The body was too decomposed for a visual ID, but it was covered with the shawl Jessica was last seen in.

Who else would it be?

She wasn't just dumped on the logging road. She was buried and lovingly covered. Someone had taken a lot of time and great care to dispose of her body, leading Ash to believe that the individual knew her and lived somewhere nearby. Nobody would just stumble onto that road unless they were familiar with the area.

Which meant the girls were close.

There were a few houses scattered up there, most of them off-the-grid hunting retreats, but with darkness closing in, it was too dangerous to continue the search. Ash wanted to canvass them all first thing in the morning, and Zak planned to be right there with him, whether or not the grumpy bastard liked it.

Bella had saved him when he hadn't even known he wanted to be saved. It was only right he returned the favor.

"Ugh, I need to shower off the smell of decay," Anna said as they walked into the house. "It's making me nauseous. Can you feed the dogs?"

"I got it." He nodded to the stairs. "Go on up."

He fed Winston and Ranger, slipping them an extra treat each because they were such awesomely good boys. Then he went out to the barn to check on the residents of C-Wing. Even though Anna hadn't asked him to, he knew she'd sleep better knowing everyone was safe and tucked in for the night.

By the time he got back to the house, he found Anna curled up in bed in just her robe with a towel still wrapped around her wet hair. Sound asleep.

He leaned over to kiss her, but thought better of it when he caught a whiff of himself. The scent of death clung to him, too. He detoured to the bathroom.

When he crawled into bed beside her ten minutes later, naked and still damp from his quick shower, she moaned softly and turned toward him. He kissed her and unwound all that gorgeous copper hair from her towel with one hand while the other walked down her belly to the apex of her legs.

Her eyes opened a crack, and she smirked at him. "What are you doing? I'm trying to sleep."

"I'm trying to make you come."

She arched against his hand. And, moments later, she did come. He caught her cry of pleasure with his mouth, swallowing it down as he eased himself over her. Her legs opened around his hips, and he sank into her sweet heat with a groan.

The sex was slower than usual. Less frantic. Less desperate. He wanted to touch and taste and explore every inch of her body. He wanted to *feel*. Her. Everything. It only seemed right after facing the ugliness of death head-on like they had. He even let her explore him and trace her fingers over his scars—which he still struggled with. He hated he wasn't still the smooth-skinned boy she'd once loved.

"Will you ever tell me where these came from?" she murmured against one scar before kissing it.

"Maybe. I don't know." He pushed his hand into her hair and watched, mesmerized, as the red stands filtered through his fingers. "You don't want to know."

She propped herself up on her elbows. "I don't want you to relive the pain. That's the last thing I want. But just know if you need to talk about any of it, all of it—I'm here. I'll listen."

"It's ugly. The man who did most of it was... twisted. Askar. They broke him long before I showed up, in ways even I can't imagine. And when they set him loose on me, he... played. He was a cold sonofabitch, but he enjoyed ramping up the pain until I passed out just so he could wake me up and start it all over again."

She squeezed her eyes shut and pressed her lips to his scar again. Tears dropped onto his skin.

"Anna, don't cry." He lifted her chin with his hand and was surprised to see rage rather than pity.

"There are too damn many ugly people in the world who have only one goal: to make everyone else as ugly as they are." She crawled up his body, kissing each scar along the way. When she reached his mouth, she bit his lower lip in a punishing tug. "You will not let Askar succeed in making you ugly."

"I think he already did."

"I'm not talking about your scars or your leg." She rubbed a hand over his stump and a thrill heated his blood. His cock lengthened against his stomach, and she wrapped her fingers around it, teasing him with a loose fist. "Those things make you beautiful because they mean you survived. You survived and came back to me. So, stay with me now."

"I'm with you."

"Are you? Because you've spent the last two years going back to him, letting him make you ugly. Tell me you won't go back there again."

"Never again."

"And you're staying here with me now."

"Yeah." The word came out strangled.

"Good." She tightened her fist and dropped her mouth to his tip, sucking like a damn vacuum. His spine arched off the bed as he exploded hard enough to see stars burst behind his closed eyelids.

When he returned to himself, she wore a self-satisfied smirk.

He scowled at her. "You're evil for mixing therapy with sex."

"Sex is therapy."

He burst out laughing.

"What?"

"Just—" He gasped and clutched his ribs. He couldn't breathe and, for once, it wasn't because of a panic attack.

Eyes sparkling, she sat up. "What's so funny?"

"Thinking about how awkward that'd make group if sex really was therapy."

She laughed and flopped back to the bed. "I bet Dr. Firestone's a dominatrix."

"Oh, Jesus." He pushed his fingers into his eyes. "Nope. Don't want that mental image."

As their laughter died away, she snuggled in beside him. "We should try to sleep. Tomorrow's going to be a long day for us both."

He pulled the blanket up over them and kissed her forehead. Several long minutes ticked by in comfortable silence and her breathing evened out, but he knew she wasn't asleep yet.

"Do you think..." He hesitated.

"Hm?"

"Could you love someone like me? With all my baggage?"

Her lips curved against his neck. "I already do."

chapter
twenty-eight

DAWN WAS JUST BREAKING over the mountains when Zak climbed out of the driver's seat of Anna's Kia at the bottom of the logging road, where the search party had set up a base camp.

Ash glowered at him. "You're not supposed to be driving."

"Anna was sleeping. She's exhausted, and I wasn't going to wake her." He opened the back door to grab his backpack and let Ranger out. "You want to arrest me for caring about your sister?"

"I'll arrest you for breaking the law."

"Yeah, well, wait until after we find the girls."

Ash grumbled something under his breath and continued divvying out assignments to his deputies. When he finished, he swung onto a sheriff's department ATV. "Zak, with me."

"Aw. Does this mean we're pals now?"

"I don't trust you by yourself." His scowl deepened when Zak grabbed another ATV from the waiting group instead of climbing on the back of his, but he didn't offer further protest. He just turned the vehicle toward the mountain and gunned it.

Zak whistled to Ranger, who hopped up onto the seat in

front of him. As he hit the gas to give chase, Ranger's tongue rolled out and his lips pulled back in a grin. Crazy mutt was just as much of an adrenaline junkie as he was.

They caught up to Ash as he pulled up to the first place on their list—a rustic cabin that offered little in the way of amenities, judging by the outhouse in the side yard.

"Charming," Zak said.

Ash ignored him and went to the door, rapping on the wood with the knuckles of one hand while the other stayed close to his gun. "Sheriff's Department."

No answer.

Zak told Ranger to stay, then swung off the ATV and circled the house until he found a dusty window. He scrubbed at the grim with his sleeve and cupped his hands around his eyes to peek in. The cabin was a single room, and it was empty. "Hey, Ash? Nobody's been home for a long time."

Ash grunted, but also came over to look in the window. He scratched the cabin off their list, then shoved the paper back into his pocket and tucked the pencil behind his ear. "We're walking from here."

"Joy."

"Hey, you choose to be here. Stay close." He turned on his flashlight and, without another word, walked into the gloom of the forest behind the abandoned cabin.

Hours passed as they trudged through the woods in silence. Any conversational attempt Zak made was shut down with one of Ash's growls of annoyance, so he focused all of his attention on Ranger. The dog seemed to catch a scent near a large, expensive house perched on a cliff overlooking the ocean. He was very interested in the driveway and, nose to the ground, followed the trail into the woods. After a short walk on a path wide enough for a vehicle, they emerged onto—*well, would you look at that?*—the old logging road.

Ranger sat and glanced around, signaling he'd lost the scent, but it didn't matter.

Zak consulted his compass and a map of the area, tracing his finger along the road until he found the house. They were on the other side of the mountain from base camp, but the crime scene was only a short drive uphill from where he stood. Someone had driven from that house to drop the body up there.

"Zak!" Ash's angry voice boomed through the trees, startling a flock of birds into the air. "I told you to fucking stay close."

He winced and pocketed the map. "Why does it feel like I'm a kid disobeying daddy dearest?"

Ranger chuffed.

"Yeah, you're right. He's an asshole." He turned to head back toward the house, but spotted Ash striding through the trees, all but steaming with rage.

All right. Enough of this bullshit. They were working toward the same goal here and wanted the same outcome. The least they could do was work together like mature adults, but apparently that was too hard for Ash.

The man had been spoiling for a fight for weeks, so Zak would give it to him. "What's your problem with me?"

"You really have to ask?" Ash got in his face. "You're a drunk and a menace to my town."

"*Our* town."

"Oh, fuck you." Ash shoved his shoulder, but he'd been braced for it and didn't move, which only pissed the guy off more. "Since when have you ever cared about this place? You left us and never looked back until you had to."

Surprise burned through Zak's annoyance. Of all the things he'd expected Ash to call him out on, leaving town as a teenager had been nowhere on the list. "Is that it? You're seriously pissed at me because I left, and you were stuck here?"

"I wasn't stuck. I stayed for my family and my community. I stayed because Anna needed me after the baby—" He broke off and his eyes went wide as if he realized he'd said too much. He backed up a step. "Forget it."

"Whoa, whoa. Hold up. Baby?" Zak grabbed his shirt to keep him from taking another step back. "Anna was pregnant?"

Ash wouldn't meet his gaze. "The baby died. Stillborn."

Unease slithered through him and balled into a tight knot in his gut. "When?"

"It doesn't matter."

"It fucking matters to me. I—"

A bullet hit the tree behind them, splintering bark, and they both dove for cover behind a rotting log on the side of the road. Ranger yipped with fear and darted into the woods.

"Ranger!"

He didn't come back to Zak's call and disappeared from sight. Fuck. The dog hated loud noises and especially hated the crack of a gun.

"Who the hell is shooting?" Ash demanded and pulled his service weapon. "Did you see him?"

"No. It came from the northeast. Do you see Ranger?"

"No."

"Give me your back-up piece."

"You're on probation. I'm not giving you a gun."

"And I'm not sitting here without a way to defend myself!" He realized his voice had gone high and panicked and sucked in a breath. His hand shook as he held it out. "Please. I was defenseless in Afghanistan. I couldn't do anything but wait for them to come torture or kill me, and I never knew which it would be. I *won't* be that helpless again."

"Fuck," Ash muttered after a beat and pulled a compact pistol from his ankle holster as a deep voice, full gravel, rumbled through the trees.

"Trespassers will be shot."

"You missed, you crazy fuck," Zak called.

Ash hissed between his teeth. "Jesus, do you have to antagonize everyone?"

"I don't miss," the man said. "If I wanted you dead, you'd be bleeding out at my feet. Get off my property. This is your only warning."

Ash holstered his gun and stood, hands raised. "It's just me and my friend Zak."

Oh, so they were friends now? When the good old rule-following sheriff had been about to punch him moments ago? Okay.

Ash smacked him and said through his teeth, "Stand up." Then he turned back to the man and calmed his voice. "We're out looking for a couple of missing girls. Their mother was murdered. Her body was found yesterday uphill from here."

"On my property?"

"No. State land."

Zak rose from behind the log. The man, in full camouflage and face paint, lowered his weapon slightly. He was younger than expected, early to mid-thirties, and held himself like a soldier. His face was obscured by the paint and the shadow of his boonie hat, but the shape of it was wrong, like he'd been broken apart and glued back together wonky.

"So get the fuck off my land. No girls here."

"What about that house on the cliff?" Ash lifted his chin in the direction of the place. "Do you know who owns it?"

"Some fucking company rents it out to rich tourists."

"Have you seen anything strange over there in the past few weeks?"

"I mind my own business."

"Okay." Ash slowly reached into his coat pocket and pulled out the missing flyer. He held it out, but didn't move forward to give it to the guy. "These are the girls, Bella and

Poppy. If you see them, please contact me and not the man listed on the flyer. It's urgent. Whoever killed their mother is still on the loose, and we just want them safe."

After a tense moment, the man inched close enough to grab the poster, then backed up fast. He stared at the pictures, then crumpled the flyer and stuffed it in his pocket. "Leave."

"Yeah, we're going." Ash grabbed Zak's arm and hauled him back toward the house.

"Two men looking for you girls."

At the gravelly voice, Bella jolted awake and spun around, making sure Poppy was still asleep and tucked in safely behind her.

"Get away from us!" Instead of sounding tough like she'd hoped, her voice came out too high and wobbly. "I have a gun!"

"No, you don't." A man materialized like a ghost at the front of the lean-to.

She blinked at him. No, that wasn't possible. People didn't just appear out of thin air.

He carried a rifle on his shoulder and was dressed head-to-toe in camouflage, blending in with the foggy greenery of the morning. She couldn't see his face behind the layers of paint. "Who are you?"

"You're on my land." He held out a gloved hand, and she flinched back.

Growling low in his throat, he dropped whatever he'd been about to hand her. It floated to the ground, and she saw her own face staring out from under the words HAVE YOU SEEN US? Poppy's picture was there next to hers. Both photos were years old, from when they lived in Tucson. She picked the poster up, scanned the text, and saw Jake's name and number at the bottom.

She dropped it like it was on fire. "We're not going back."

The man grunted. "Can't stay here."

Of course she knew that. When she ran from the house two nights ago, she'd originally thought to take Jake's car, but he'd locked the doors and she didn't dare go back inside for the keys. She'd run for the road, figuring it had to lead somewhere—only to walk and walk and get nowhere. When headlights shone through the trees, she dove back into the woods because it had to be Hoodie Man returning. No way it was anyone else. This place was too remote for a random passerby.

The first night, she and Poppy had huddled under a redwood with a hollowed-out trunk, cold and exhausted. She tried to convince Poppy it was a fun adventure, but the girl wasn't stupid.

"Who was that man?" she kept asking between hiccupping sobs. "Who was that man? Why did we run? I want to go back and watch *Lilo and Stitch*!"

"Shh." Bella held her close and rocked her. "He's nobody. He's gone, but we can't go back."

Poppy stuck her thumb in her mouth. "I'm scared."

She couldn't admit that she was, too. She was the big sister. The protector. Nothing was supposed to scare her, so she'd curled around Poppy, offering her body heat, and waited until morning.

As night brightened to day and day faded to evening, she finally accepted they were lost. They had to go back to the house, or they would die out here, but she was so hopelessly turned around, she couldn't find her way back.

The lean-to seemed like a gift from God when she found it. It had three walls built with thick logs and a sturdy roof. There was a fire going in front of it. Inside was a sleeping bag and backpack filled with bottles of water, some kind of jerky wrapped in a canvas bag, and two shiny apples. It looked like someone planned to return at any second. At that point, she hadn't cared if that someone was Jake or Hoodie Man.

But the lean-to didn't belong to either of them.

It was this guy's.

"I'm sorry we ate your food."

He grunted.

"And drank your water."

He glanced to his right, and she noticed a spot on his face where the paint had smeared away. Her breath caught in a gasp. He was horribly disfigured under all that make-up, his skin thick and ridged.

At her squeak of shock, he looked back at her, and his lips flattened into a scowl. "There's a dog here. Follow him. He'll take you to safety."

And then he was gone again, ghosting off into the trees.

Zak shook off Ash's grip and spun on him once they'd put a good amount of distance between them and the crazy man. "Who the fuck was that?"

Ash scrubbed a hand over his beard. "Shane Trevisano. He lives off the grid up here and doesn't like people coming around."

"Obviously."

"He's harmless."

"He *shot* at us," Zak reminded. "Jesus, I gotta find my dog."

Ash shoved a hand against his chest, stopping him from going back into the woods. "Like he said, if he wanted to hit us, he would've. He was a Navy SEAL. He won't hurt Ranger, but he will sure as shit shoot you if you trespass again."

Zak's throat burned. His lungs constricted as panic sizzled around the edges of his consciousness. "I can't lose that dog."

"We'll find him," Ash said, gentling his tone. "And, for fuck's sake, breathe. I can't have you passing out on me at a crime scene."

"Crime scene?" He glanced around and realized they were at the edge of the house's yard again. He tried sucking in air, but it kept getting caught on the lump in his throat. "That house—Ranger found a scent trail—"

"Yeah, pretty sure the girls were held here. I found a partial footprint in blood on the porch. It's small, like a petite woman's or a child's. I'm calling everyone in to focus our attention here. You good?"

Fuck, no. His ears buzzed and his head felt stuffed with cotton from lack of oxygen, but he nodded so that Ash would step back and give him some space.

Ash turned toward the woods. "Ranger!" His voice boomed like thunder. "Come, boy!"

Zak bent double and focused on breathing until the buzzing stopped, then he straightened and cupped his hands around his mouth. "Ranger! It's okay, mutt. It's safe now. C'mon, buddy! Come back—"

Ash grabbed his arm in a vise grip. "Holy shit. Look."

He spun and spotted his dog trotting toward them, looking very pleased with himself. And for good reason, because on the trail behind him?

Two pale, dirty, terrified girls emerged from the woods.

chapter
twenty-nine

BELLA LATCHED on the Zak's hand as soon as she was close enough to touch him and her eyes spilled over with tears. "Thank you for finding us."

"Hey, no big deal. I owed you."

She nodded and refused to let go of his hand even as paramedics treated her and her sister for some minor cuts and dehydration. He couldn't tell if she actually recognized him from that foggy road or if she just saw him as her protector now.

Either way, he didn't mind, and stayed with her through the police questioning at the sheriff's department. She proved to be a perfect witness and described everything, starting with the night her mother was murdered.

Had she seen the shot that killed Jessica?

No, she'd heard it.

Could she describe the man who kidnapped her?

Yes, but there were two guys, and one of them was Jake Beckett. She claimed he was a pedophile who had abused Poppy back in Tucson.

Ash easily tracked down and arrested the bastard at the local hospital, where he'd been admitted for a severe concussion. Jake wasn't talking, but Bella had described his accomplice— "Hoodie Man," as she'd called him—to a sketch artist and a BOLO went out. If he was still anywhere in town, he'd be found.

Once it was all done, Ash and Zak left the girls in the comfortable interview room used for victims and their families. Ash leaned against the wall and called his sister on speakerphone to update her.

"Oh my God," she whispered. "What those poor girls went through..."

Zak watched them through the window. They were curled up together on the couch, with Poppy twisting one of Bella's dreadlocks around her finger. "What happens to them now?"

Ash scrubbed both hands over his face. He looked exhausted. "CPS is looking for a foster home. Until then, they'll go into a group home."

"No," Anna said, outrage ringing in her voice. "Absolutely not. They're coming here."

Ash sighed heavily. "AJ, you said you couldn't take more placements after the last adoption fell through—"

"I know what I said, but I'm still a foster parent in the eyes of California, and those girls have gone through too much to get shoved into a group home and forgotten. I'll contact my social worker. Bring them here."

Of course she was a foster parent. It was perfectly on-brand for Anna Jade Rawlings, the queen of lost causes.

And, with that decision, the girls were finally safe.

So why couldn't Zak breathe properly? Each inhale tightened his chest with dread as he pulled her car into the driveway.

Anna waited on the porch swing with a book in hand, and he was thrown back in time fifteen years to that summer day he'd come looking for Ash and instead noticed her as a woman for the first time.

Everything had been so innocent then. So easy.

How he wished he could go back.

Anna tossed her book aside and raced down the porch steps, Winston on her heels. She threw herself into his arms before he was fully out of the car. "You found them!"

"Ranger did." At his name, Ranger clambered across the seats and shoved his nose between them.

Anna laughed. "You both did." She backed up long enough to let Ranger jump out of the car and run with Winston, then wrapped herself around him again and raised her face toward his for a kiss.

Goddammit, he wanted to kiss her. He wanted to wrap his arms around her and bury his face in her neck to breathe in her comforting scent.

He didn't move.

Now that the adrenaline of the day was fading, the words Ash said out in the woods kept bouncing around in his skull.

The baby died. Stillborn.

Ash's truck rumbled up the driveway behind them. He had the girls with him. There was no time for the conversation they needed to have now, and Zak couldn't decide if he was relieved or anxious that it had to wait.

Anna drew back, her forehead creased with worry. "What's wrong?"

"Once you get the girls settled, we need to talk." He watched her eyes as he spoke and saw the flicker of panic.

Oh, yeah. She knew exactly what was wrong. His heart froze in his chest.

Fuck.

A car door opened. She abruptly broke away from him and turned to meet her brother and the girls, her smile of welcome overly bright.

Ash recognized the strain in it and glowered at Zak as he opened the Tahoe's back door for Bella and Poppy. Of course

Ash thought it was his fault. The guy would never consider the possibility that something he had said was causing her current distress.

Anna ignored them both and focused on the girls. "Hi, I'm Anna. You'll be staying with me for a bit while we figure everything out, okay? You'll be safe here." She set her hand on her dog's head. "And this big guy here is Winston. He's very friendly. You can pet him if you like."

Poppy looked up at her big sister with hope in her exhausted eyes.

Bella nodded and nudged her toward the dog. "It's okay."

"Hi, Winston." She squealed with delight when he lapped his tongue over her face. "He kissed me!"

"He likes you," Anna said.

Bella's flat, assessing gaze traveled over the yellow house to the barn. "I hear a lot of dogs in there."

"That's because I run a rescue and we train dogs to do special things like find people."

Poppy beamed. "Like Ranger! He found us."

"Yep, just like that. Zak and Ranger work here."

He scoffed at her choice of words. *Work?*

She glared at him, made a cutting motion with her eyes, and guided the girls toward the house. "I'll take you out to the barn to meet some of the other dogs, but let me show your rooms first. Are you hungry?"

Yeah, okay, Zak thought as he trailed them. Work was not the word he'd use to describe his current situation, but how else did you explain a DUI and court order to a five-year-old? He had no idea. He'd never had kids.

That he knew about.

The baby died. Stillborn.

Ash caught his arm. "I know what you're thinking. Forget I said anything. Don't take her back there."

Zak shook him off and strode into the house. As angry as

he was at Anna, he wanted to make sure the girls were comfortable.

He found Bella upstairs in the room that used to be Ash's. She stood in the center, looking lost, like she wasn't sure what to do next. Anna's and Poppy's voices flowed out of another room down the hall.

He tapped a knuckle on the doorjamb. He didn't want to startle her. "How are you doing, kid?"

She spun toward him. "Honestly? I... don't know. What's going to happen to us?"

Tehani had asked him the same thing the first time he spoke to her after his rescue, except the conversation had been in Pashto.

"What's going to happen to me?"

"You'll be okay. I'll make sure of it."

"Promise?"

He cleared his throat to ease the sudden tightness. "Listen, I knew a girl who was a lot like you. She was in a horrible situation with no way out, but she escaped through grit and stubbornness. Just like you did."

Bella rubbed her arms like she was cold. "Is she okay now?"

Jesus. He didn't even know. He assumed Tehani was happy in her new life, but he hadn't spent enough time with her since coming home to know for sure.

But Bella needed reassurance and so he forced a smile. "She's amazing now. She was adopted into a loving family. She's safe and happy."

It probably wasn't a lie. His family loved Tehani. He knew at least that much was true.

Bella studied him for a long moment. "I didn't want to say anything with everyone else around, but... I recognize you from the highway. You almost drove your bike into my van, but veered off at the last minute. You tried to kill yourself."

He winced. He should've seen this coming. "Yeah. I was in a bad place that night."

"I'm glad you survived."

"Bella!" Poppy sprouted through the space between his leg and the door like—well, a poppy—and wrapped her arms around her sister's legs. "Anna says we can have ice cream tonight after dinner. Ice. Cream." She emphasized each word with wide-eyed solemnness. "She even says we can even have any flavor we want, and she'll make her brother go to the store for it."

Bella smiled down at the girl, affection lighting up her world-weary face. "That sounds amazing. What flavor are you getting?"

"Hmm... just vanilla. No, wait. Chocolate! No, strawberry."

"You know there's a flavor that has all three?" Zak said. "Neapolitan. That's my favorite."

His metal knee thunked hard on the floor when he knelt to meet her gaze and Poppy looked at it, then up at him. "Does that hurt?"

"Poppy, that's not nice," Bella chided.

He held up a hand. "No, it's okay. She's allowed to be curious." He pulled up his pant leg and showed her his prosthetic, tapping his fingers against the metal. "My old leg hurt a lot more."

"What happened to it?"

He felt Anna's presence in the hallway behind him like a static charge on the back of his neck, but ignored her, keeping his focus on Poppy. "Well, see, I hurt it really, really bad when I was a soldier, and it got so infected that it was making me very sick, so the doctors got rid of it to save me."

Her blond brows slammed together. "Were you mad? I think I'd be mad if someone took away my leg."

"Yes, I was mad at first, but now I'm glad they did it because I wouldn't be here to meet you if they hadn't."

Anna made a soft noise behind him that sounded like a muffled sob.

Poppy looked at her, then grinned at him. "I'm glad, too." She took his hand and tugged. Her fingers felt so tiny and fragile wrapped around his palm. "Are you having ice cream with us?"

"Absolutely." He pushed to his feet. "I never turn down ice cream."

Later, after the bowls were all but licked clean and the girls settled into the living room—Poppy lounging in front of the TV using Winston as a pillow, and Bella browsing Anna's vast collection of books—Zak took Anna by the hand and led her out to the porch.

She made sure the door was firmly shut, then turned to him with a sad smile. "You're good with them."

All he could do was shake his head because the lump that had been in his throat all day suddenly made speech impossible. Several seconds passed in silence before he forced any words out. "The baby was mine, wasn't it?"

She wrapped her arms around herself and nodded once. Tears spilled down her cheeks. "Ash told you about her?"

Her.

A baby girl.

He squeezed his eyes shut as pain unlike anything he'd ever felt cleaved his heart in two. "Why didn't *you* tell me?"

She didn't answer.

"If she had lived, would you have told me about her?"

Again, she said nothing, but she didn't have to. Her silence was answer enough. She had never planned to tell him about his daughter.

"Fuck." He shouldered past her and yanked open the door, whistling for his dog. "Ranger, c'mon. Let's go."

"Zak, wait." She reached for him, but he swatted her hand aside and put as much distance between them as he could. He was so angry, he was afraid of what he'd do if she touched him.

"Stay away from me."

"Zak!" She chased him down the porch steps, but skidded to a halt when he whirled on her. She must've seen how close he was to the edge of doing something unforgivable, because she flinched back.

"My community service ends today," he said through his teeth. He actually had twenty-four hours left in his sentence, but he couldn't do it. Not with her. "You'll sign my papers saying I served the entire hundred hours, and then we're through."

She shook her head. "Please, don't do this. Let me—"

"We're. Through."

chapter
thirty

"ARE YOU OKAY?"

Anna shut and locked the front door, then swiped at her eyes and forced a smile as she turned to face Bella. "Of course."

The smile hurt her face, and she knew her cheeks were probably a splotchy mess from sobbing.

After Zak walked away, she grieved all over again for her daughter—the precious baby with a head full of spiky black hair that she'd only gotten to hold for a few hours. She grieved for the other children she'd never have because the birth had been so traumatic the doctors had to remove her uterus to keep her from bleeding to death. She grieved for the decisions she'd made as a scared teenager and for the relationship she'd just lost because of those decisions. And, most of all, she grieved for Zak, because she knew him, and this could push him over the edge into complete self-destruction.

If something happened to him tonight, she'd never forgive herself.

She called Ash to let him know Zak might go off the rails, but he didn't pick up. She didn't leave a voicemail. He'd call back.

And then she pulled herself together and went into the house because the girls she'd taken in needed her to be strong.

Bella eyed her doubtfully, then the door. "You don't have to pretend for me. I heard a little of that fight. It sounded intense."

She exhaled a shaky breath. There was no fooling this girl. She'd seen too much in her young life. "It was, but I'll be okay." She just hoped Zak would be, too. She pushed that thought out of her mind and peeked into the living room to check on Poppy. The little girl was sound asleep in front of the TV, still using Winston as a pillow. The dog's tail slapped the floor when he saw her watching. He was in his happiest of happy places.

She noticed Bella had left a stack of books on the end table untouched. "Didn't find anything that interested you?"

Bella's cheeks flushed with color, and she dropped her gaze to the floor. "Uh... there was a book I was reading before—" She broke off and picked at a loose thread in the sleeve of her borrowed Lost County Sheriff's Department hoodie. "Mom ripped it up when she found me with it and called it smut—but it really wasn't," she added quickly. "There was some kissing, but that was all. I swear it wasn't anything bad—"

"Bella." Anna set a hand on her shoulder and waited until she lifted her gaze. "You're sixteen and I imagine, given the life you've lived, you're well aware of what sex is. If you want to read a romance novel that shows a healthy sexual relationship, you're allowed to in this house. In fact..." She dug her phone out of her pocket and brought up the Amazon app. "What's the title?"

Bella told her.

She found it and had to admit it looked good. She'd always loved fantasy and would definitely read it once Bella was done. "There. Ordered."

Bella's eyes rounded. She looked at the phone and then back at Anna. "Just like that?"

"Just like that. You'll have it in a couple of days."

To Anna's shock and delight, Bella lunged forward and hugged her tightly. "Thank you for being so nice to us."

She wrapped her arms around the girl and every emotion roiling inside her settled. This was good. This was right. Whatever other bad decisions she'd made in her life, sheltering these girls was not one of them.

They stood together like that until a knock on the door had Bella pulling back and swiping at her face with her sleeve. "Who's that?"

Zak?

Anna squashed the stupidly hopeful thought. It wasn't him. He was probably well into his first bottle of Jameson by now.

"I bet it's my brother. I called him a little while ago." She pulled open the door and started to ask Ash why he didn't just use his key—

Not Ash.

Not Zak.

She froze at the sight of the gun pointed at her head.

"Hey, Sheriff. You haven't left yet?"

Ash looked up from his computer and had to scrub at his gritty eyes before he could focus on the deputy in his doorway. "Uh, no." He cleared away the rasp in his voice and checked his watch. Almost midnight. He'd been going for nearly forty-eight hours on only a brief nap. No wonder he kept seeing spiders on his desk that weren't there. "Just finishing some things. What do you need?"

The deputy hesitated. "You should go home and sleep."

He mentally fortified himself for another twenty-four on the clock and reached for his coffee. The mug was empty. He'd need at least a gallon more. Better yet, he should just mainline the stuff right into his veins. "C'mon, Wright. I'm already here, so you might as well tell me."

"Jake Beckett escaped his guards at the hospital," Wright said. "We're looking for him, but thought you should know."

"Shit." He set the empty mug down and reached for his phone, seeing a missed call from his sister. He called back, but it dumped straight into voicemail.

It was fine, he told himself. She was probably sleeping. Besides, she had Zak there. The man was a pain in the ass, but he was combat trained. If Jake tried anything crazy to get to the girls, Zak would protect them with his life. Of that, he had no doubt.

"I want every available deputy out hunting his ass down. And someone should swing by my sister's—no, never mind. I'll do that." He grabbed his coat off the back of his chair.

"One other thing before you go," the deputy added. "We officially have an ID on the body from the logging road up near Razorrock Falls."

"That fast?"

"Yeah, I forwarded the results to your email. Her DNA was on file."

Ash spun back to his computer and pulled up his inbox. "I expected as much. Jessica Lowe has been arrested multiple times and—" His gaze landed on the name. "Wait. Is this correct? The victim's name is Nicole Madison?"

"Yeah, that's what the report said. Her DNA was on file because fifteen years ago, her one-year-old daughter, Makyla Madison, was kidnapped from a shopping center in the suburbs of Boston. Nicole and her husband, Kyrone, both gave DNA samples after it happened in case remains were ever found."

"And were they?"

"No. The girl is still considered missing to this day."

"So she'd be sixteen now..." He scattered papers on his desk, looking for Jake Beckett's flyer. When he found it, he held it up next to Nicole Madison's ID on his screen.

Holy. Shit.

The resemblance was undeniable.

Bella Lowe was actually Makyla Madison.

ANNA RAISED her hands and backed up. "I don't have any money."

The wild-eyed blond woman nudged her back into the house with the tip of the gun. "I don't want money."

Bella gasped and her face drained of color. "Mom?"

Jessica Lowe smiled and reached for her. "Hi, baby."

"But you—you—" Bella stumbled backward until she hit the stairs and collapsed onto the steps. "You were dead. I saw you dead..."

"Oh, that wasn't me, honey. That bitch Nicole was spreading lies, trying to take you away from me."

Keep her talking, Bella.

Anna tried to will the command at the girl as she inched toward the kitchen. Ash insisted she have a gun for protection, but she never thought she'd actually need it and kept it in a lockbox on the top shelf of the pantry. If Bella could distract Jessica long enough, maybe she could get to it.

Keep her talking.

As if hearing the silent plea, the girl glanced at her, but the quick movement drew Jessica's attention.

She swung around, eyes showing too much white and

bugging out of her head. Her pupils were pinpricks. "Don't move!"

"Mom!" Thinking fast, Bella popped to her feet and grabbed the woman in a hug. "I'm so glad you're alive, but what are you talking about?" Her eyes pleaded for Anna to run. "Who's Nicole?"

Brave, brave girl.

Jessica wrapped her arms around Bella. The gun wobbled dangerously in her hand. Her finger was still too close to the trigger. "She's nobody. A liar. I had to kill her. I was just protecting you like any good mother—"

Anna darted for the kitchen and almost made it. Her fingers were inches away from the pantry door when Jessica grabbed her ponytail and yanked her head back, shoving the gun against her temple.

"And now *this* whore's doing it, too!"

The woman's breath was hot and rancid on the side of her face. Anna gagged. Her scalp was on fire, and her neck felt like it would snap if pulled any harder. A strangled cry of pain escaped her throat as Jessica yanked her hair again, and the gun bruised her temple. With her neck at such an extreme angle, she couldn't breathe. She flailed for something—anything—to use as a weapon, but her hands found nothing as she was dragged back toward the foyer. Her vision grayed around the edges. Voices floated around her, sounding miles away.

"Mom, please stop. You're hurting her."

"She's trying to steal you. I saw you hugging her. You're *my* daughter!"

"Yes, yes, I am. I'm your daughter. I don't even know this woman. She was just letting us stay here for the night because we thought you were dead. But you're not, so let's get Poppy and go home to the camper."

"We don't live in the camper anymore. I have a house for us. Where's Poppy?"

"In the living room."

The grip on Anna's hair loosened, and she sucked a ragged gasp into her burning lungs. Jessica shoved her toward the living room. Her legs didn't want to work right, knees going to gelatin, which pissed the other woman off.

Winston had backed Poppy into a corner and stood guard in front of her. The golden didn't have a mean bone in his body, but he was putting on a good show. He looked vicious.

Good boy.

"Get it away from her!" Jessica shrieked and pointed the gun at Winston. "Get it away from her!"

"It's okay, Mom." Hands held up in a calming gesture, Bella put herself between the gun and Winston. Which was either extremely stupid or very brave since her mother was high on something and not thinking rationally. Her finger could slip on the trigger at any moment.

Bella took Winston by the collar and led him into the half-bath off the living room. He howled the moment the door clicked shut. "Okay, the dog's gone. Please put the gun down. You don't need it now." She crossed to Poppy and scooped her up. "We're going with you."

For a half second, Jessica seemed like she'd comply, but then she tightened her grip on Anna again. "So's she."

Bella's eyes popped wide in surprise. "Why?"

"Don't you talk back to me like that!" Jessica struck her in the face with the butt of the gun. The blow was quick and brutal, and she dropped Poppy.

The younger girl screamed.

The older just straightened slowly with the faraway look of someone pushed beyond their limit. She pressed her sleeve to her bleeding nose. "I wasn't trying to be sassy, Mom. I just don't want her to come. We don't need her. We have you."

"You stupid cow. Don't you know anything? Her brother's a cop. She'll call him as soon as we leave."

Bella met Anna's gaze, but only for the briefest of seconds. Still, it was enough to convey what she was trying to say. *I'm sorry.*

It's okay, Bella. She wanted to shout it, but kept her mouth firmly shut and hoped the girl could see the reassurance in her eyes. *We'll be okay.*

Searching for Rachar

chapter
thirty-two

"SHE HAD no right to keep the baby a secret."

Ranger cocked his head and watched Zak pace circles around the house with a bottle of Jameson in hand. He'd opened it as soon as he got home, but had yet to drink a drop.

"*No* right. Right?"

Ranger chuffed an agreement.

He pointed at the dog. "Yeah, exactly. I'm not in the wrong about this." He noticed the bottle in his hand and lifted it to his mouth, but stopped before drinking and paced some more. "You know my ex-wife was pregnant once?"

Ranger woofed.

"Yeah, crazy, right? Our marriage was shit at that point, but, man, I wanted that kid more than anything. She miscarried pretty early on. We never even had time to tell our families."

Ranger sighed and settled down on his bed, eyes still tracking Zak's every movement until he stopped pacing. He slid down the living room wall to sit next to his dog and finally remembered the Jameson in his hand. He tilted his head back and opened his throat. The liquor burned all the way down to the knot in his gut.

He waited for the numbness to set in.

It didn't.

His rage was too hot, his sorrow too sharp.

"A daughter," he whispered and knocked the back of his head against the wall with a solid THUNK. "I had a daughter. Jesus, she'd be Bella's age now. I wonder if she looked like me or Anna. Did she have a name? She must have a name. Is she buried somewhere?" He pressed his fingers to his burning eyes. "Fuck. I have to know where our baby's buried. I have to go back and talk to Anna."

Ranger lifted his head and thumped his tail at her name.

"Yeah, I know you're excited to see her again, but I don't know if I can talk to her without completely losing my shit. How do I talk to her after what she did? Not telling me..." He stared off into near space, imagining teenage Anna in a hospital bed with a stillborn baby in her arms. His heart clenched so hard he gasped at the pain and worried for a moment he was having a heart attack.

It was late, but he had to talk to her tonight. He wouldn't be able to rest until he had answers.

He struggled to his feet, cursing when his knee locked up.

"C'mon, mutt." He grabbed his truck keys, only to remember Ash had booted the damn thing. He dropped the keys back on their hook by the door. "Okay, guess we're walking."

He knew the instant he set foot on Anna's road that something was wrong. Red and blue lights bounced off the low-hanging clouds at the top of the hill.

Police.

He broke into a run, cursing his prosthetic every step of the way because he wasn't as fast as he used to be. Fuck waiting on the VA to process his claim for a new leg. He was buying himself a running blade because he planned to run and hike all over these mountains with Anna next summer.

With Anna?

He stumbled at the thought and had to catch his breath.

Yes, with Anna. When he pictured his future, he couldn't imagine life without her and the dogs. He couldn't hate her when she'd been a frightened teenage girl not much older than Bella—the same age as Tehani was now—making big, hard choices that even adults had trouble with.

Jesus, why all the police? Was she hurt? Were the girls?

He picked up his pace.

Ash stood on the cordoned-off street in front of his sister's house, barking out orders to his deputies.

Zak grabbed his arm. "What's going on? Where is she?"

"Fuck," Ash said with deep disgust and yanked out of his grasp. "You've been drinking."

Yeah, but he was stone-cold sober. "Where is she, Ash?"

"We don't know. We think Jake Beckett has her and the girls."

"Why?"

"How should I fucking know? My job is to find my sister, not get into that creep's head and—" He stopped. Took a breath. "Sorry. Uncalled for. Beckett escaped the hospital, and he might be working with Jessica Lowe to abduct the girls."

"But she's dead. We found the body..." At Ash's uncompromising glare, he trailed off. "Didn't we?"

"The body wasn't Jessica."

Zak rubbed at the headache drilling into the center of his forehead. "Still doesn't make sense. Why would Beckett work with her? He was desperate to find the girls and get them away from her. He said she kidnapped them."

"It's a clusterfuck and I can't get into it now." A deputy called out to him from Anna's driveway, and he shouldered by Zak. "Just stay out of the way. I don't need your drunk ass stumbling around the crime scene."

Yeah, well, too bad. Zak wasn't drunk, and he was absolutely going to stumble around until he found out what the hell was going on. He stopped by a deputy's car, the bright red headline of Bella and Poppy's missing flyer catching his attention. A whole stack of them sat on the dashboard. He surreptitiously reached through the window and grabbed one.

Jake Beckett's number was listed at the bottom.

He walked away from the crowd and pulled out his phone. He didn't expect an answer and figured he'd leave a voicemail, but a deep voice said, "Hello?"

Thrown, he took a minute to collect his thoughts. "Beckett?"

"Who's asking?"

No, not Beckett. This voice was too deep to belong to the man he'd met at The Grove and also had a bit of a Boston accent.

When he didn't reply right away, the man said, "I'm hanging up."

"You're Hoodie Man."

He didn't hang up, but his silence confirmed Zak's suspicions. "This is Zak Hendricks. Is Beckett with you?"

More silence.

"Okay, answer me this. Did Jake ever hurt Poppy?"

"He never touched her. That was one of Jessica's many lies."

Another suspicion confirmed. "I assume you know Jessica has taken Bella and Poppy again, and I think she also has the woman I love. Maybe we can help each other."

The phone went dead, but he knew they hadn't hung up. The time counter still ticked on the call, so they'd put themselves on mute. Probably discussing whether or not they should trust him.

He waited.

Every second felt like an eternity.

Finally, Hoodie Man came back. "What's your plan?"

"I'll meet you at the intersection of Rawlings Road and Highway 1."

"The sheriff—"

"Isn't paying attention to us."

He growled. "If you're setting us up..."

"I'm not."

The line went dead again. This time, because they had ended the call.

Ranger pushed his head under Zak's hand.

"Yeah, mutt. I hope I'm making the right call, too." He looked at Anna's house. Ash still stood at the end of her driveway, deep in conversation with two of his deputies. He sucked in a breath and glanced back the way he'd come. It was a long trip back to the highway. Depending on how far away Beckett and Hoodie Man were—and he had to assume they were close by—he had little time to get back down there. He'd have to run.

When he got to the intersection, a car already idled in the scenic pullout across the highway from Anna's road. He jogged to it and pulled the back door open for Ranger.

Jake Beckett sat in the backseat, looking like he would either throw up or pass out at any second. He still wore a hospital gown over a pair of baggy sweatpants. A line of stitches marched across his forehead over his right eyebrow.

The light-skinned black man in the driver's seat was huge. His hands made the steering wheel look like a kid's toy. And he was indeed wearing an Army green hoodie.

"You got a plan, Hendricks?" he asked.

Zak slid into the empty passenger seat. "You got a name other than Hoodie Man?"

"Kyrone Madison. Ky."

"Yeah, Ky. I have a plan. Jessica spent a lot of time at the Palace, so we're gonna go knock heads there until somewhere tells us where on the mountain she's holed up."

Ky grinned. "Now we're talking."

thirty-three

THE HEAD-KNOCKING WASN'T as satisfying as Zak had hoped.

Jake stayed in the car because one: he was a wanted man, and two: he was in no shape to fight. But when Zak and Ky shoved into the bar, the drug-addled roaches who infested the place scattered.

Ky snagged one skinny, pock-marked guy by the back of the neck before he could scurry away, and pinned him to the wall. "I saw this asshole with her the night she killed my wife."

The guy's eyes bounced around in his skull like ping-pong balls. "I don't know nothing."

Zak got in his face and studied every oozing scab, then smiled and drew his gun. It wasn't a friendly smile, and the asshole practically shit himself. "Yeah, you know something. Tell us where Jessica is, and we'll let you walk out of here on the legs God gave you." He pressed the boot of his prosthetic on the guy's foot and the barrel of the gun to his kneecap. "Or... I can tell you in excruciating detail exactly how much it hurts to get shot in the knee right before we put bullets in both of yours. You want two of these shiny metal legs?"

"I—I—" He screeched and flapped his arms wildly like a wounded bird. "She's on the mountain."

"We know that much, asshole." Ky knocked him against the wall again. "Where?"

Five minutes later, they slid back into the car with the location, but Ky didn't start the engine right away.

"We good?" Jake asked.

"We know where they are." He pushed out a breath and tilted his head toward Zak. "Because this guy is wicked scary." The Boston really came out of him in those words. "*I* nearly pissed myself."

"You held your own," Zak said.

"Been in more than my fair share of fights." He finally started the car and glanced over at Zak. "I never got a chance to thank you for finding my wife. I hated leaving her like that —" His voice broke, and he cleared his throat. "But I didn't have a choice."

They had a bit of a ride ahead of them. Plenty of time to get the truth.

"What happened?" Zak asked. "I want the whole story. I think I've earned it."

Ky lifted his gaze to the rearview mirror.

Jake nodded, then winced and touched his stitches. "We should tell him. He's in this now."

"Yeah, okay." Ky exhaled hard. "The girl you know as Bella? She's my daughter, Makyla. She was taken from us when she was a year old. My wife was out shopping and turned away for just a second and..." He snapped his fingers. "Gone. There was video footage of the kidnapper, but we never found her."

"Until recently," Zak guessed. "Jessica Lowe?"

"Yeah. About two years ago, we met Jake at a conference for parents of kidnapped children and he showed us a picture of his missing girls. I recognized Makyla instantly. She looks just like my wife, but with my nose and smile."

Zak studied his profile in the darkness. Yeah, he saw it now.

"So, we started working together," Jake continued. "When I tracked Jessica here, I contacted Ky and Nicole."

Ky shook his head. "Should've gone to the police, but I'm a felon, ya know? Work in tech now, but did five years for some dumbass shit I got into as a kid. I don't got much trust for law enforcement."

"It took him a year to trust me," Jake said. "Even though I lost my detective's shield before we met because I was so obsessed with finding my girls."

Zak shifted to look at the guy in the backseat. "Poppy is your and Jessica's biological daughter?"

Jake forgot about his concussion and nodded, then groaned and squeezed his eyes shut, leaning back in the seat.

Ky glanced back at him. "If you're gonna boot again, open the window."

After several deep breaths, he said, "No. I'm good." He straightened and met Zak's gaze. "I met Jess at a bar in Tucson six years ago. She was gorgeous and fun. A little dangerous, but I liked that about her. It was a fling, but then Poppy came along, and I fell in love with both girls. Not so much their mother, but I asked her to marry me, anyway. We never made it to the wedding. She became erratic, got heavily into drugs. The last straw was when she hit Bella hard enough to break one of her teeth. I immediately filed for custody, having no idea Bella wasn't actually her daughter. She started screaming that I was a pedophile, then took off with the girls when I was granted custody. I put my life on hold to find them, and finally tracked them here last month."

"When Jake told us he knew where they were, Nic and I flew out here," Ky said. "We confronted Jessica at the campgrounds. We demanded she give Makyla—Bella—back to us. She lost it, pulled a gun. I tried to wrestle it away from her, but she shot Nic—" Again, he stopped and cleared the thick emotion from her throat. "Jessica got away, and I couldn't call the police. The optics weren't good. A black felon standing over a white woman's body with two kidnapped girls yards away? Hell, they would've shot me on sight. So I took the girls up to the house we'd rented, then buried Nicole, and called Jake for help."

Jake picked up the story: "We decided to keep the girls locked in the house until we found Jessica, and I started riding the sheriff to look for them because I knew if he looked long enough, he'd find Jess for us. But I got sloppy. Stupid. I just wanted to see my girls again so badly and Bella—that girl's a fighter." He laughed softly and touched the line of stitches. "She believed her mother's lies about me and she'll do anything to protect Poppy. As soon as she saw me, she charged. Knocked me flat out and ran. I couldn't have been prouder of her. Or more scared for her. We looked all over those woods, but she kept Poppy well hidden until you and your dog found them."

Zak stayed silent for several moments, processing it all. "Wow." It was the only thing he could think to say.

"Jessica's unstable," Jake added. "Unpredictable. She was diagnosed with borderline personality disorder and is almost certainly self-medicating with narcotics. Whatever our next move, we have to proceed with extreme caution because she *will* kill the girls rather than let them go."

chapter
thirty-four

BELLA USED every trick she'd ever learned to keep her mother calm. Submission. Flattery. Nothing was too low if it kept Anna and Poppy safe.

Poor Anna. She'd been nothing but nice and didn't deserve to be knocked out with a gun and stuffed her into the trunk of her own car.

"Bella, you drive. I'll tell you where to turn." Jessica slid into the backseat with Poppy, the gun on her lap, and directed her to drive up the mountain to a ramshackle trailer perched on a narrow spit of land between two pot fields.

The smell of weed clogged the air and turned Bella's stomach as she got out of the car. "Where are we?"

"Our new home," Jessica said brightly and swung out her arms to encompass the property. "These fields are ours, too. We're homesteaders now."

Bella stared at the trailer, and the churning in her stomach got worse. The roof didn't even look waterproof. "It's perfect."

"I wanna go back to Anna's," Poppy said around her thumb. "She had ice cream and TV and dogs."

Jessica swung around, face red. "You don't need any of that shit—"

Bella deftly stepped into her path before she could attack Poppy. "Thank you, Mom. You worked so hard to give us this. I'm so proud of you."

"I *did* work hard. You know how many disgusting cocks I had to suck—"

"I know."

"Ungrateful little bitch." She sneered at Poppy, but turned toward the trailer, and her eyes went all dreamy, like she was looking at a mansion and not a piece of shit on flattened wheels. "Come see. It's huge. You both have rooms. Your own rooms!"

Bella glanced back at the car as Mom dragged her up the crumbling concrete stoop to the front door.

God, she hoped Anna was okay.

Anna was pissed.

When she woke up bouncing around in her own trunk and realized what had happened, she literally saw red for the first time in her life. The anger was so hot she was surprised she didn't burn right through the bottom of the trunk and land in the street. She braced herself to keep from whacking her head on the roof and breathed through the rage, but the air in the confined space was getting thick and too warm.

She was suffocating.

No. There was enough air. She just had to relax and breathe. When the car stopped moving, she could free herself.

Finally, the car stopped.

She heard voices—Bella's and Poppy's for sure, and probably that bitch Jessica's, too—but couldn't make out what they were saying. She waited, biding her time until she was sure they'd moved far enough away, then found the inner trunk latch.

Sweet, cold air rushed in. She let herself take a second to breathe before pushing the trunk all the way open. She crawled out and crouched by the car, making a mental note of the trailer and the cannabis fields. She could see Wildcat Ridge peeking through the trees to the southeast, which helped orientate her. She wasn't that far from home. She could run back and get help for the girls.

She edged toward the road. She was barefoot, and rocks bit into the bottom of her feet, but she kept moving one slow step at a time. Once she got to the road, out of sight of the trailer, she could run and find Ash.

Nearly... there...

Headlights speared through the trees and cut off abruptly. Someone coming to the rescue?

She froze and debated her options. There were a lot of unfriendly people up here. Whoever was in that car was probably in league with Jessica. Best to avoid.

She backed away and crouched in the pot field to wait and watch. Several dark shadows left the vehicle and tiptoed through the looming trees. She counted three people, most likely men given their sizes, and... was that a dog?

Shit. If it scented her, she was done for. She had to move downwind—

The dog stepped into a spear of moonlight and her heart swelled with relief as yellow eyes focused on her position. Ranger raced toward her, licked her face, then tore back to Zak, then came back to her, leading him straight to her just as he'd been trained.

"Anna!" he whispered and grabbed her in a tight hug. He kissed her, and that sweet sense of relief evaporated.

He smelled like alcohol.

She would never fix him, would she? He'd always go back to the bottle at the slightest bump in the road, and she'd been a fool for thinking she could change that. Sometimes a lost cause really was completely, irredeemably lost.

The realization had tears springing to her eyes.

"Hey, don't cry. I'm here now. You're safe." He swiped the tears away with his thumbs, careful to avoid the swelling lump on her cheek where Jessica had hit her. "Where are the girls?"

Unable to speak, she tilted her head toward the trailer.

He looked at the thing, then nodded to the two men with him. One was Jake Beckett, still dressed in a hospital gown. The other looked like the sketch Bella had provided of the man who kidnapped her.

She stared at the three of them. "What...?"

"Long story," Zak said. "But they're friends. This is Ky and you know Jake. They only want the girls safe."

"So," Ky said, crouching down, trying to make his enormous body small. "What's our next move?"

Zak looked at the trailer again. Several seconds ticked by in silence.

"I'll lure Jessica out," Anna said. She hadn't even realized she'd had the thought until the words were coming out of her mouth, but she knew it was a good one. "While she's distracted, you guys get the girls to safety."

"Anna, no—"

She whirled on Zak. "Do you have a better plan?"

His lips compressed into a thin line.

"Okay, then." She didn't give him the chance to protest and started toward the house, picking a two-by-four off the ground on her way. "Be ready to move."

The window in the trailer's front door shattered in an explosion of glass.

Anna.

She must've gotten out of the trunk somehow.

Bella tried to get in front of her mom, but Jessica was like a train when she got like this, single-minded in her anger. There was no stopping her.

Jessica tore from the trailer, and three gunshots exploded through the night air.

Fuck, fuck, fuck.

"What was that?" Poppy asked.

Bella pushed her sister down behind the musty couch. "Stay here, Pop. Keep your head down." Grabbing a knife from the dingy kitchen, she ran to the door with absolutely no plan whatsoever until she emerged onto the concrete stoop and saw Anna, weaponless, facing off with her mom.

"Let the girls go, Jessica."

"I won't let you steal them from me, you cunt!"

God, Mom was going to shoot.

Bella was only a few steps behind and saw Jessica's finger tightening on the trigger. She had to do something and raised the knife, plunging it down with all her strength. It stuck in the flesh of her mom's shoulder and the blow jarred up her arm, making her stumble. It didn't go as deep as she expected and didn't stop Jessica at all.

Mom screeched and spun toward her with the blade still protruding from her back. It was like she didn't feel the pain. Her wild eyes flashed with betrayal as she raised the gun. "Why, Belladonna? Why would you hurt your mother like that? All I ever did was love you."

Bella raised her hands in defense. If Mom came any closer, she'd punch and kick and bite to get free. "If you loved me, you never would've hurt me. Real moms take care of their kids."

"I *am* a real mom! I took care of you the best way I knew how."

"Yeah, well. It wasn't good enough." She'd think later that antagonizing the crazy lady with the gun was probably not the best idea, but, in that moment, she was done placating. "I hate you. Poppy hates you. You *suck* as a mother."

Several things happened all at once in a frenetic blur of movement. The gun exploded. Someone screamed—was it her voice? Anna's? Jessica's? Or maybe all of them at the same time. She flinched back, braced for pain, but none ever came, and a huge shadow dove in front of her, pulling her to the ground.

Hoodie Man.

At first, she thought the bullet had missed them both, but then he coughed, and blood sprayed from his mouth.

No, no, no.

Bella touched his face. Yes, he'd kidnapped her, but he'd been kind and gentle—which was more than she could ever say about her mother. He wrapped an enormous arm around her and dragged himself close, using his body as a shield as the bullets kept coming in a frenzied spray. Even injured, he was still trying to protect her.

Who *was* he?

Another man in a hospital gown appeared from the woods and charged at Mom.

Jake!

He got a hold of the gun, and, for a moment, it looked like he was going to win the fight. But his strength faded fast, and Jessica twisted out of his grasp. Hatred warped her pretty face into something deformed and ugly as she shoved the barrel against his head and pulled the trigger without a second's hesitation.

"They are *my* girls!" Jessica screeched as he fell lifeless at her feet. She kicked his body. "Mine. Mine. Mine! You shouldn't have tried to take them from me. They belong with me. And you—" She whirled on Anna, who had taken cover behind the car when the bullets started flying. Zak was there now, too, holding his dog's collar with one hand while shielding his girlfriend with his body.

Jessica pulled the trigger again.

The gun clicked.

Zak grinned and rose to his feet. It was a mean smile. If Bella hadn't seen for herself that he was a good man, she would've been terrified of him.

"Ranger," he said coolly. "Attack."

A dog-shaped bullet slammed into Mom's side. She tried to shake him off and when that didn't work, she tried to hit him with the butt of the gun. He ignored the blows and lunged, his teeth ripping open her cheek and nose. She dropped the gun and clutched her face with a haunting wail of agony, and it was enough of a distraction for Zak to grab her from behind. He shoved her to the ground and sat on her, his metal knee pressing into her back. She shrieked and flailed, but it was useless.

"Good dog," Zak said, breathing hard. "Good mutt."

"Bella!" Anna flew to her side and pulled her out of the bloodstained dirt, patting her down, looking for injuries. "Oh my God! Where's the blood coming from? Where are you hurt?"

"I'm okay." But as she spoke, she realized she didn't sound okay. Her voice was hollow. She shook her head and stopped Anna's frantic inspection, clasping the woman's hands in her own. "No, really. I'm okay. It's not mine." She nodded to the man on the ground. "It's his. He saved me."

Hoodie Man.

But his hoodie was dark and sticky with so much blood now.

She let go of Anna and knelt next to him. He was so familiar, and not only because she'd spent three weeks as his captive. It was a visceral familiarity like she'd always known him. "Thank you."

He coughed and blood bubbled up from his mouth to splash on his chest. "Had... to... protect you."

"Why?" She studied his face. His dark, almond-shaped eyes glazed over with pain. His full lips tried to smile for her, but twisted into a grimace instead. The shape of his nose was—

Oh.

She touched her own nose and suddenly realized why his features were familiar. She saw them every time she looked in the mirror.

Her heart pounded painfully hard and tears she couldn't control burst from her eyes as she reached for his hand. "Are you my dad?"

"Yes." His smile was like hers, too, but now it was bright red with his blood. "I've been looking for you for fifteen years, Makyla."

chapter
thirty-five

ZAK WATCHED the coroner pull a sheet over Jake Beckett's body and swallowed back an unexpected rush of emotion. The man had only wanted his girls safe. That was all any father wanted.

True, the girls *were* safe now. Jessica was going to prison for a long time, so maybe Jake thought giving his life for it was an acceptable trade-off.

Zak shifted his attention to the departing ambulance as its siren blasted through the night. They were rushing Ky to the high school football field for a life flight to the closest trauma center two hours away. He might not survive. His blood pressure had already crashed once while they were loading him onto a stretcher.

Jesus.

Zak pressed his fingers to his eyes, but Ranger wasn't about to let him mope and shoved that big wedge head underneath his arm, looking for pets. He laughed softly and hugged the dog.

Yes, there had been a lot of bloodshed tonight, but it was over. Bella and Poppy were safe. Anna was safe.

Anna sat with the girls while they gave their statements to

police, but then had to let them go with CPS. He could see the heartbreak all over her face as the social worker's taillights faded into the darkness.

She would've been an excellent mother.

It pained him that she never got the chance. And that he never got the chance to see if he was any good at being a father. Would he have given his life for his daughter like Jake and Ky had for theirs?

Yes.

Without a doubt.

He never met her, but he'd trade places with her in a heartbeat if it meant she'd be alive and happy now.

And he wanted to meet her.

He walked over to where Anna sat in the back of another ambulance, a blanket draped over her shoulders. "Where's our daughter buried?"

She pulled the blanket tighter around her and squeezed her eyes shut. "Can we not do this right now?"

"I need to know."

She pushed out a breath. After a long moment, she looked at him with sad, exhausted eyes. "In the family cemetery on the hill behind the house."

"Did you give her a name?"

"Bella," she whispered and stared at the empty road as if she could will the social worker's car to reappear. "Her name's Bella, too."

Oh, shit.

He swallowed down a messy mix of anger and grief, but it stuck in his throat. "You should've told me about her the moment you found out you were pregnant."

In a burst of anger, she popped to her feet and squared off in front of him. "Yeah, but what would you have done differently if you had known?"

"I don't know. You never gave me the chance to figure it out."

"Well, *I* know." She pushed against his chest. He didn't move. "You would've done exactly what you did when your ex-wife miscarried. Nothing. You just kept right on going like nothing happened, nothing changed."

The words accomplished what her push hadn't. He took a step back. If she had stabbed him in the heart, he would've been less surprised. "How do you know about that?"

"I was friends with Jillian, remember? She came home for a bit after the divorce and she knew what I'd gone through with my baby, so we bonded in our grief."

"Did she know...?"

"No, she didn't know the baby was yours. Nobody knew. I never named the father. But she told me how you ran off to another war zone when she miscarried, and it only reaffirmed that I'd made the right call by not telling you."

"That's not—I didn't run. I was deployed and couldn't say, 'no, sorry, my wife just miscarried, and my marriage is in shambles. Maybe next time.' That's not how the military works, and Jillian knew that when she married me."

"Yes, she did. But it wasn't the deployment that killed your marriage. You avoided her calls for six months. You can't tell me you were surprised when you got home, and she served you with the divorce papers."

"I wasn't, but—" He stopped short and took a second to calm himself. This wasn't going well. "No, we're not talking about that. We're talking about us."

"There is no us. You made that quite clear before you stormed off to go drink yourself to death."

"Anna, I didn't—"

When he reached for her, she backed away, hands up in defense. "No, stop. I can smell it on you. I signed your community service papers earlier tonight. You're free, but if you're so determined to kill yourself, I'm not letting you adopt Ranger. He doesn't deserve your bullshit after clawing his way back to life. He needs an owner who wants to live. You're too dangerous."

Zak didn't bother telling her that Ranger had enjoyed every second of the danger tonight. He'd loved rescuing the girls. *That* was what had breathed life into him. And he loved cadaver detection. His yellow eyes shone with excitement whenever he caught a scent. His tail didn't stop wagging the entire time his nose was to the ground. He needed that purpose in his life.

So did Zak.

And now she was taking it away from them both.

He snatched the leash from his belt and knelt in front of his dog. Ranger watched him with worried eyes as he clipped the leash on. He rubbed the dog's ear and his throat closed up so he couldn't say any of the things he wanted.

You saved me.

I love you.

Both of you.

He glanced over his shoulder at Anna. She'd turned away, but only halfway. Tears tracked silently down her cheeks.

Ranger pushed his wet nose against Zak's cheek, and it was only then he realized he was crying, too. He swiped at his face with the back of his hand and hugged Ranger for a lot longer than he'd intended.

He didn't want to let go.

Eventually, Anna gave a light tug on the leash, and he stood, letting Ranger go to her side. He couldn't look at them as he walked away, but Ranger's questioning whine sent fresh spikes of pain through his heart.

Anna was right. The dog would be better off. He was too much of a disaster to take proper care of him.

Hell, he could barely care for himself.

She'd find a good family to adopt Ranger. Maybe he'd even land on a ranch with cattle to herd. He'd love that way more than sitting around watching Zak drink.

He'd be fine.

Question was, would Zak be okay without him?

chapter
thirty-six

ZAK SCOWLED into his beer as Ash took the stool next to him. "Checking up on me, *Ashley*?"

He wasn't drunk enough to deal with the man right now.

In fact, he wasn't drunk at all.

When he'd walked into the Mad Dog and signaled to Rose for a beer, he'd had every intention of getting shit-faced and forgetting the entire night. But the beer had sat in front of him since it arrived, untouched, sweating onto the cocktail napkin. He had zero urge to drink it.

"Actually, no," Ash said and glanced toward Rose. "I just stopped in for a drink on my way to check on Anna, but I'm glad to see you're staying out of trouble. We've had enough of that tonight."

The urge to ask about Anna was overwhelming, so he asked about Bella and Poppy instead. "How are the girls?"

"Scared, sad... but coping. They're at a hotel with one of my deputies tonight and will go into foster care tomorrow."

"With Anna?" There he went, asking about her anyway. He couldn't help himself. Dammit.

Ash shrugged. "That's for CPS to decide, but I think they'd be stupid not to let those girls stay with her."

Zak agreed wholeheartedly. Poppy was an orphan now, and Bella might end up one if Ky died. And even if he survived, would he be in any shape to care for a traumatized teen? The girls would need a lot of love and patience to work through this experience, and Anna had both qualities in spades.

"Any word on Ky's condition yet?"

"Still in surgery," Ash said. "When he went in, the doctors were hopeful he'll live. Whether he'll walk again is another story. The bullet damaged his spine."

"Damn."

"What you three did was dangerous, reckless, and probably illegal." He waited a beat for Zak to meet his gaze. "But thank you for saving my sister."

Zak glanced away and picked up his beer. "I fucked things up with her," he muttered and set the glass down again without drinking. "And I don't know how to fix it."

"For one thing, you don't need this." Ash grabbed the beer and downed it in several long gulps. He made a face and set the glass down with a thunk. "Ugh. Warm as piss. How long have you been sitting here?"

"Hours," Rose said from behind the bar. "Get him out of here, Sheriff. He's brought the whole place down with his mood, and I'm about to close."

"No, I'll walk." Zak pushed up from the bar and, just like the last time he was here, his prosthetic caught on the stool's legs. He stared at it for a second, then shook his head and pulled it free. "I was gonna get a new one of these things so I could hike with Anna and the dogs without it locking up on me."

Ash watched him fit the leg back into place. "You still should. Get a new leg. Go for a hike. Get a new dog. You don't need Anna to live."

Zak snorted. "Easy for you to say. You've always had her

right by your side since the day you were born. What would *you* do without her?"

Ash stayed silent.

"Yeah, exactly." He paid for his beer and left Rose a generous tip to make up for all the times he'd stiffed her. "See you around, Ash."

Back at home, Anna cleaned the blood off Ranger, gave him and Winston an early breakfast, and then, finally, let herself break down. She collapsed on the couch in her trashed living room, and that was where her brother found her sobbing hours later.

"Oh, AJ." He scooped her up and hugged her. "It's all right."

"They might not let me foster the girls now," she said between sobs.

"I know."

"I couldn't save Zak, either. I was a fool for trying."

He winced. "I feel like that's my fault. I shouldn't have mentioned the baby, but he was pissing me off and I spoke without thinking."

She wiped at her face. "So you always knew Zak was her father?"

Ash squeezed her against his side. "Of course I did. You really thought you could run around with my best friend for an entire summer and I wouldn't notice? I could see the little hearts dancing around your head every time you looked at him."

"You never said anything."

"Because he made you so happy. And you made him

happy. I thought it was a good thing. I stupidly thought you two were meant to be."

She bumped him with her shoulder. "Back when you still believed in silly things like love."

"What can I say? I was a dumb kid."

"You can be a dumb adult sometimes, too." She shook her head. "I always wondered what happened between you and Zak. Couldn't figure out why you suddenly hated him when you were always like this." She twisted two fingers together, then sighed. "It's so obvious now, but I never put the pieces together."

"He hurt you. More than that, he destroyed you."

"No." She ducked out of his arms and faced him. "He hurt me, yes, but it was no different from any other teenage girl getting her heart broken for the first time. Under other circumstances, I would've moped for a bit and then moved on. Teenage love isn't meant to last, and I would've realized that. I *did* realize that, and never held it against Zak. You forget he was just a kid, too. No, what destroyed me was losing my baby, and he had nothing to do with that. He didn't even know she existed until today."

"So if you forgive him for breaking your heart, why push him away now? He loves you. And, as much as it galls me, I know you love him."

Anna looked down at Ranger and Winston, snuggled side-by-side in Winston's bed. "Because he was drinking again tonight. If he doesn't love himself enough to stay sober, how can I trust him to stay alive? I can't watch him self-destruct. That would destroy me."

Ash popped to his feet and paced for a few minutes, then stopped in front of her, hands bladed on his hips. "Okay, I'm probably going to regret saying this. He went to the Mad Dog tonight."

She rolled her eyes. "Of course he did. Was he drunk and disorderly?"

"No." He held up a hand, stopping her. "Zak had one beer in front of him that he hadn't touched. He's not the same man I dragged out of that pub this summer, and I know that's because of you and Ranger. You think you can't save him, AJ, but you already have. Don't give up on him now."

BY THE TIME Zak walked the five miles home from the Mad Dog, dawn lightened the sky over the mountains to the east.

It had been a long night.

One of the longest of his life.

The only other night that had lasted longer was after his rescue when he was in the hospital in Germany waiting to see whether he'd keep his leg. He'd thought his life was over then.

And now Ky would face a similar night.

He'd have to talk to the guy, offer a shoulder to lean on. A night like that could fuck you up for years.

Something moved across his porch as he approached and he stopped short in the driveway, tensing until the animal came into the light.

Yellow eyes.

A smile spread across his face. "Hey, mutt. You miss me?"

Ranger wagged his whole body.

A car pulled into the driveway behind him. He didn't have to turn to know it was Anna. He always knew when she was nearby.

"Hi," she breathed. "Ranger escaped again."

"I see that." He turned to her. Her eyes were red and puffy from crying, and the bruise on her cheek had turned a deep, ugly purple. "Can't keep him away from me."

She ran a hand along the top edge of her car door. "Maybe... we shouldn't."

His chest swelled, but he didn't dare give in to the hope. "What are you saying?"

She shut the door and came toward him, stopping with only inches between their bodies. She laced her fingers with his. "Let's go visit our daughter."

The grave was so much smaller than he expected, the headstone just a simple plaque in the ground with the name Bella Elyse Rawlings carved on its smooth surface. Anna had recently left fresh flowers, and she bent to clear away some of the fallen petals.

She gazed up at him. "Here she is."

Jesus. It hurt so much more than he expected. He knelt in the grass and pressed his hand against the cold stone. "What did she look like?"

Anna pulled a slim photo album from her jacket pocket and sat beside him. "I have pictures if you want to see her."

"Yes. Please."

She handed him the album.

He opened it and wasn't sure if the sound that escaped him was a laugh or a sob. "Jesus, she looked like me. Look at all that hair."

"She had your lips, too. That pout." She reached over his arm and turned the page, pointing to a close-up of the baby's face. "She was beautiful, wasn't she?"

He exhaled. "Yes. Too beautiful for this world."

"Maybe that's why she couldn't stay." Anna covered his hand with hers. "I love you so much. It was a mistake not telling you about her sooner, but I can't change the past. I can only hope you'll forgive me, so we can try for a future."

"God, Anna." He set the album aside and pulled her into his arms. "I've already forgiven you. I love you, too, and want a future with you more than anything."

She stiffened. "You should know I can't have more kids."

He rubbed her back in soothing circles. "Then we'll adopt. Dogs. Kids. We'll take them all in. I already know of two girls who desperately need a loving home." He looked at the gravestone again. "And I think our Bella would approve of having another Bella around here to watch over us. I mean..." He met her gaze again and pushed her hair back from her face. "If you want me to stay."

Her smile was dazzling. "Of course I do. Why wouldn't I?"

"Well, I don't know, you might want to foster me first and see how it goes before you make that commitment. I'm a bit feral." He growled, doing a fair imitation of Ranger, and lowered his mouth to hers. "You might have to housebreak me."

"Mm." She returned his kiss. "Can I swat you with a rolled-up newspaper when you do something wrong?"

He pulled back and stared at her in mock horror. "You'd never do that to a dog."

"Because even the worst dog I've ever met is better behaved than you."

"Fair point." After another kiss, he pushed to his feet and held out a hand to her. "Now let's go rescue our girls and bring them home."

epilogue

One Year Later

"SO, does anyone want to start today?"

When nobody else immediately spoke up to answer Dr. Firestone's question, Zak opened his mouth, but no words came out. He rubbed his sweaty palms on his pants and Alfie the Psychic Dog trotted over to dance in front of his chair. He picked the dog up and nuzzled those soft ears, taking comfort in the contact.

Thank you, he told Alfie silently, then blurted to the group, "Last night was the one-year anniversary of the night I tried to kill myself."

Donovan gave a low whistle. "Zak Hendricks coming in hot. You gotta warn us when it's gonna be one of these heavy sessions, man."

Everyone ignored him.

"What did you do?" Dr. Firestone asked, shifting in her seat to face him. "Did you mark the occasion in any way?"

"Yeah, I went to my parents' house for dinner. It was the first time in... I don't even know how long. Anna and the girls went with me."

Dr. Firestone smiled. "How'd it go?"

He drew a breath and thought back to dinner. His dad hadn't seemed to know how to talk to him and his mom wouldn't stop fussing over Anna, Bella, and Poppy. He let his breath out in a whoosh. "It was awkward at first, but actually wasn't too bad. I spent so much time pushing them away, I forgot I love them. I've missed them. We're going to have dinner over there more often—once a month to start, so we can all get to know each other again. They really enjoy having more grandkids to fawn over."

"What do the girls think of them?"

"Bella was reserved. She's still having a lot of trust issues, so she kept them at arm's length. I hope that will change the more she's around them. But Poppy?" He chuckled. "She reveled in their attention and already has Dad wrapped around her little finger."

"That little girl has *everyone* wrapped around her finger," Sawyer said with a big grin. "Including you, Hendricks. She's gonna be a heartbreaker."

Zak winced. "Believe me, I'm well aware. I'm already stocking up on rifles and ammo to keep away asshole teenage boys."

"Weren't you the king of asshole teenage boys?" Donovan said.

Horror bloomed in his gut at the thought. "Oh, Jesus. She better not bring home the teenage version of me." He'd need a lot more ammo. Were chastity belts still a thing?

"And what about your siblings?" Dr. Firestone asked, deftly steering the conversation back to the topic at hand. "Were they at dinner?"

He wiped a hand down his face and shook his head. "Uh, no. They're all less forgiving than Mom and Dad. I have a lot further to go with them—especially with my brother, Taj—to prove I'm in this for the long haul."

They'll come around, Pierce signed. *Even Taj.*

He nodded. "I know they will, and I don't blame them for their reluctance to accept the new and improved me. I haven't given them much reason to trust me over the last few years. Or, honestly, even before that. I've always kinda been a shitty brother to them, and I've been downright cruel to Tehani."

"Tell us about that," Dr. Firestone said. "Why do you think you were so much worse with her?"

He closed his eyes. Damn, this hurt to admit. "Because every time I looked at her, all I could think was, *this is your fault.*"

"But she'd just a kid," Sawyer said. "What were you blaming her for?"

"My life and the shitty way I thought it turned out. I shouldn't have pinned any of it on her, but after I saved her over in Afghanistan, it felt like I lost every-fucking-thing while she got this whole new great life. It hurt to see her happy, and I hated her for a long time because of it. But last night, I finally apologized. She forgave me." He snapped his fingers. "Just like that. I know an apology doesn't make up for the way I've treated her, and I still catch myself slipping back into that ugly mindset, but I'm doing my best to connect with her. It's part of this whole new year, new me thing I'm working on."

"Speaking of new you," Donovan said and nudged his prosthetic with the toe of his boot. "Nice shiny toy you got there."

"Yeah, you like? I can run, hike, ski—hell, even rock climb with this. It's awesome." He pulled up his pant leg and kicked the blade out for everyone to see.

Well, everyone except Sawyer, who could maybe see it if he wiggled it around a bit? He still wasn't sure how the guy's superpower worked.

He dropped his pant leg and took a moment to smooth it down over his prosthetic. He'd been looking for an opening to bring up the idea that had been itching at the back of his brain for weeks, and figured now was as good as a time as any. "So... guys? I have a proposition for you."

"I'm flattered, man," Donovan said, "but you're not my type."

Zak ignored him. "Something Veronica said during my first session with the group has stuck with me."

Veronica glanced around, uncertainty in her dark eyes. "What did I say?"

He nodded to Zelda, snoozing comfortably beside Sawyer's chair. "You said you wanted a Zelda. At the time, I thought you were ridiculous for thinking a dog could help you." He stroked a hand over Alfie's head. "But then I met Alfie, who is a better therapist than any human. No offense, Doc."

Dr. Firestone grinned. "None taken. I happen to agree."

"And then Ranger changed my life in ways I couldn't have imagined at this time last year. He gave me love I didn't know I needed and a purpose I didn't know I was missing." He tilted his head toward the door of the community room and the lobby beyond it. "There are a lot of dogs out there that need people, and a lot of people in here that need purpose. That purpose could be a fast-response tactical K9 unit— search and rescue, narcotics detection, disaster response, and more. We could create that here at Redwood Coast Rescue. We have the skills."

"But won't that be expensive?" Sawyer asked. "With Anna still fighting Monarch in court, where would we get the money for it?"

"We'll have to do a shit-ton of fundraising."

I'm in, Pierce said.

Donovan patted the air in a slow-down gesture. "Hang on. We're all broken, busted, used up pieces of trash that the military threw away, and you want us to become a doggie A-Team?"

Dr. Firestone sighed. "Donovan, we've talked about this. You're not broken or trash."

"Am I still a Marine?" When nobody answered, he nodded. "Yeah, so what good am I?"

"There's more to life than being a Marine," Sawyer said. "And maybe this project of Zak's is exactly what we need to prove that to ourselves. I'm in, too."

"Me, too," Veronica said, surprising everyone—including, it seemed, even herself. Her eyes widened for a split-second, but then narrowed. After a moment, she nodded. "Yeah, I'm willing to try."

"Nah." Donovan pushed out of his seat and strode to the door. "I'm out."

Zak handed Alfie to Veronica, then followed. "Hey, Van, hold up. Can I show you something?"

Donovan halted, one hand on the exit. "You're not changing my mind."

"I know. But, c'mon. Humor me for a second."

Donovan grumbled, but trailed him to C-Wing. He hesitated just inside the door. "What are we doing here?"

"We got a new resident I thought you should meet." Zak motioned to the first kennel in the row. "Say hello to Spirit."

Donovan scowled at him for a long moment before scoffing and walking forward. When he spotted the dog, he recoiled. "What the fuck's wrong with her?"

A black and white border collie sat in the middle of the kennel with her head cocked at an odd angle. She wobbled to her feet, and her feathered tail swept excitedly through the air.

"She was surrendered to us because she had a brain tumor."

"Nope." Donovan nearly steamed-rolled over Zak in his haste to leave. "I've seen enough."

"You haven't seen anything yet." Zak shoved a hand against his chest, pushing him toward the door that led outside to the agility yard. On the way, he paused long enough to open the kennel. "Come on, Spirit."

Donovan watched the dog with a horrified expression as she wobbled down the hall, nearly smacking into the wall several times.

But when Zak opened the outside door and Spirit got a taste of freedom, her legs straightened, and her body stretched to its full length. She took off like a bullet and ping-ponged around the agility yard in a black and white blur.

Donovan's jaw actually fell open. "How...?"

"The brain is a mysterious thing, even in dogs. The tumor was benign, but it was putting pressure on things, causing her balance issues. We removed it, and she's been improving daily, but the amazing thing is, when she runs, a switch flips in her brain and it's like nothing was ever wrong. Sasha—"

"That the sexy vet's name? I've been wondering."

Leave it to Donovan Scott to get hung up on that.

Zak rolled his eyes. "Yes, Sasha is the rescue's vet. She believes Spirit will make a full recovery and Anna thinks she'll make an excellent search and rescue K9." He gave it a minute, letting Donovan watch the dog run, then faced the man. "So, is she trash? Should we give up on her because her brain's a bit scrambled or should we see what else she's capable of?"

Donovan growled low in his throat. "I know what you're doing, Hendricks."

"Is it working?"

His jaw slid to one side. "You bastard." He held out a hand for her leash. "I want to see what she's capable of."

Searching for Rescue

The Redwood Coast Rescue adventure continues with
Donovan Scott's book, **Searching for Risk.**

And if you'd like to see how it all started, you can read about
Zak's rescue in **Honor Reclaimed**.

For more information on Tonya's upcoming releases,
subscribe to her newsletter.

Too Wilde to Tame

9 798986 780863